The Trial of
Anna Cotman

VIVIEN ALCOCK

The Trial of Anna Cotman

Mammoth

To my sister Pat

First published in Great Britain 1989
by Methuen Children's Books Ltd
Published 1990 by Mammoth
Reissued 2000 by Mammoth
an imprint of Egmont Children's Books Limited,
a division of Egmont Holding Limited
239 Kensington High Street, London W8 6SA

Text copyright © 1989 Vivien Alcock
Cover illustration copyright © 1991 Graham Potts

The moral rights of the author and
cover illustrator have been asserted.

ISBN 0 7497 0444 6

10 9 8 7 6 5 4 3 2 1

A CIP catalogue record for this title
is available from the British Library

Printed in Great Britain
by Cox & Wyman Ltd, Reading, Berkshire

1

It began innocently enough, nearly two years ago now. Anna was not there when it started. There were only six of them at first, five boys, and a girl they hadn't wanted but had to have, because she was Jeremy Miller's kid sister. Lindy Miller was a thin, sallow child, with a gift for worming her way into other people's business.

'Snub her at your peril,' Tom Smith had warned them, for he knew Lindy only too well.

He knew she was a teller of tales and a plotter of sly revenges. A bossy girl, quick to quarrel and slow to forgive. She had run through her friends at school like a dagger, and was now hardly on speaking terms with anyone. This was unfortunate.

'You can ask one of your friends to join,' her brother had told her. 'Just one. No more.'

She could not bring herself to tell him she didn't have any friends left. Then, just as she was beginning to feel sorry for herself, a new girl arrived, like a gift from heaven. A smiling girl, with light brown hair and a round freckled face. Her name was Anna Cotman.

Lindy Miller snapped her up.

'You're my best friend,' she told Anna firmly, making it sound like an order. Or a prison sentence.

Tom Smith, who happened to be walking past, overheard her. He glanced idly at the soft, pleased face of the new girl. Poor fool. Poor daft rabbit. She didn't stand a chance. Someone ought to warn her that's a snake she's talking to. He was tempted to warn her himself, only Jeremy Miller was his oldest friend, and it was bound to get back to him. Lindy would see to that. Besides, it was too hot to quarrel.

So he shrugged and walked on.

'Are you doing anything tomorrow?' Lindy asked the new girl.

'No. Nothing,' Anna said hopefully. She was pleased to have found a friend at her new school so quickly. She and her grandmother had only moved to Redmarsh ten days ago, to live in the cramped flat above the wool shop Mrs Cotman had bought with her savings.

Last Saturday, Gran had sent Anna out to explore. 'I'd come with you, but my knee's playing up,' she'd said. 'If you see a fishmonger, bring us back some prawns for our tea.'

Anna, walking by herself, had looked wistfully at the chattering groups in the streets, at the children fishing by the river, the two girls running and laughing over the common with a yellow dog. Perhaps next Saturday, I'll have a friend to talk to, she'd thought. Now it looked as if her wish might be coming true.

'What about you?' she asked shyly. 'Are you doing anything?'

'In the morning, yes. In the afternoon I might be

6

free. On the other hand, I might not,' Lindy said. 'It depends how long it takes. I have to do – something important. I have to go – somewhere. I'm afraid I can't say any more.' She paused, waiting to be asked why, so that she could refuse to tell, but the new girl just gave a puzzled smile and said nothing. 'It's a secret, you see,' Lindy went on. 'I'd tell you if it was just me, since you're my best friend, but there's other people in it. I mean, it wouldn't be fair to them. I promised. I can't break my promise, can I?'

'No, of course not,' Anna agreed readily.

There was a short silence. Lindy looked sideways at the new girl. She hoped Anna was not going to turn out to be a soapy little saint, all white socks and sermons. There's something very irritating about virtuous people – the way they store up gold stars for themselves in heaven, and make you look bad down here. Like someone coming to tea in a clean dress when you haven't bothered to change. Who did Anna think she was?

'Well, you don't have to sound so pi about it,' she said sharply.

Anna looked bewildered. 'Pi?'

'Pi. Short for pious. Short for goody-goody little plaster saint, see?'

'I'm sorry. I didn't mean – '

'We can't all be angels, can we?'

'I'm not. I only said – '

'Some people might consider friendship more important than a silly promise.'

'But it was you who said – '

'That's right. Blame me now.'

Anna was silent. Lindy noticed with pleasure that she looked confused. That was it. Keep her in her place.

They were sitting on a bench in the school playground. It was very hot. Lindy caught sight of her brother, surrounded as usual by a group of admiring friends. She frowned. Toadies, she thought, and wished she could throw something and hit Jeremy on the nose, but she was not a good enough shot.

Her brother was a tall, good-looking boy. His hair shone as bright as a new penny in the sunlight. Tom Smith had once said that Jeremy's hair was the only bright thing that ever came out of his head, his ideas being on the dusty side. Jeremy had only laughed and cuffed Tom lightly on the arm.

I would never have forgiven him, Lindy thought. Not if he'd said that about me. Not that he would – he knows I'm clever. He knows I'd get my own back one day, even if it took a hundred years. I'm not soft, like Jeremy. Or like this new friend I've picked up –

She turned to look at Anna and found the new girl was watching her. Anna's face was no longer smiling. It looked grave and thoughtful. Lindy remembered that if she quarrelled with Anna, there would be nobody left.

'I was only teasing,' she said quickly. 'I've been thinking. Tell you what. I don't want to leave you out, seeing you're my best friend. Wait in for me tomorrow afternoon and I'll come if I can. I don't know whether I can swing it or not, but I'll do my best. Only not a word to anyone, promise?'

'I promise,' Anna said, and added, smiling. 'I can't

tell anyone, anyway. I don't know what you're talking about.'

Lindy leaned over and whispered damply in Anna's ear. 'I'm going to ask them if you can join.'

'Join what?'

'Ssh!' Lindy glanced round the crowded playground suspiciously. Then she cupped her hands so that they made a tunnel between her mouth and Anna's ear, and whispered.

'I can't tell you. I daren't. Not unless I'm allowed. They might – I don't know what they'd do. It's terribly secret, you see. I hope I did right to tell you this much. I hope you're not the type to blub and blab – you're not a coward, are you?'

'No,' Anna said, but she didn't sound any too sure about it. She couldn't help remembering that she was nervous of fierce dogs and dentists and thunderstorms. Still, she didn't see how Lindy's secret could have anything to do with these.

2

Saturday afternoon was hot and dull. The sky was curdled with clouds as grey and lumpy as porridge. Anna sat on a high stool in the wool shop, staring through the window at the people passing by outside.

'D'you think I could've missed her?' she asked.

'Not a chance,' her grandmother said. 'The way you've been watching, a fly couldn't have crept by without your seeing it. What time did she say she'd come?'

'She didn't. She couldn't promise anything. She just said she'd try to come.'

'You mean she expected you to wait in all afternoon on the off chance?'

'I wanted to. You don't understand.'

'Mmm,' Mrs Cotman said.

Anna's grandmother was a small woman, who would have been plump if she'd allowed herself to be. Her hair was reddish, a shade her hairdresser called Autumm Leaves No. 3. She was all the family Anna had, for Anna was an orphan. Her mother and father had died in a car crash when she was a baby. She could not remember them. She had a photograph on the chest of drawers in her room, but the bride and groom in the silver frame looked too young to be anybody's parents. They looked as if they were children themselves, playing at weddings. Anna sometimes put a vase of flowers in front of the silver frame, but she didn't really miss her mother and father, whom she'd never known. She loved her grandmother. They got on well together.

'You're a good girl. You're a credit to me,' Mrs Cotman had told Anna only that morning. Anna did not notice that her grandmother was frowning as she said it. Mrs Cotman had brought Anna up to be kind and unselfish. Now she was beginning to worry in case she'd overdone it. Anna was too friendly. Too soft and unsuspecting – like a fledgling who hadn't learned to fly away. The first neighbourhood cat would get her.

'I don't think I like the sound of this new friend of yours,' she said now. 'Don't let her push you around. Why can't she call for you properly, come in the door like everybody else? Walking past the window and expecting you to follow her, what sort of nonsense is that?'

'Oh Gran, I told you. She may be with other people. She's doing me a favour. She's going to ask them if I can join – ' Anna broke off.

'Join what?' her grandmother asked.

'A sort of – um – club, I think.'

'A sort of – um – club, you think?' her grandmother said. 'Anna, you're hopeless. Didn't you ask? Now you're to find out what it's all about before you go joining anything. You don't want to get mixed up with a bad crowd.'

11

'I won't. I can look after myself.'

'Said the goose to the fox. Anna, don't be in too much of a hurry to make new friends – '

'There's Lindy!' Anna cried, her face lighting up. She slid off her stool. 'Bye, Gran. Won't be late.'

Mrs Cotman went over to the shop window and looked out. She saw Anna greet a thin, sharp girl, all pointed elbows and knees. As she watched them, the girl glanced back towards the shop and grinned.

I don't like the look of her, Mrs Cotman thought, and frowned.

A woman, who had stopped to admire the purple jumper in the shop window, caught her eye through the glass and walked on hastily.

'They said, yes,' Lindy whispered, looking over her shoulder as if the street were full of spies.

'You mean . . .?'

'You can join. They didn't want to let you at first. I had a terrible job persuading them. "She's my very best friend," I told them. "If you won't let her join, then I'm sorry but I'll have to resign." They wouldn't have that, of course. I'm too important to them. I'm – ' she glanced over her shoulder again and then whispered, 'I'm the Silver Lady.'

'Oh,' said Anna, impressed, though she had no idea what Lindy was talking about.

'I went on and on at them, I did really, and in the end they said you could come.' Lindy paused, obviously waiting for thanks.

'Thank you,' Anna said.

It was all right for Gran to say find out all about it

before you join. It was too late for that. Lindy spoke as if she was already committed.

'I'm to take you there now,' Lindy was saying. 'Remember, Anna, you've got to do exactly what I say. It's important. Don't let me down.'

'Where are we going?'

'I can't tell you that. It's secret. You mustn't ask any questions. You mustn't even speak unless you're spoken to. I'm going to blindfold you now.'

Anna began to feel uneasy. She'd been through this sort of thing before and didn't care for it much. Like when she'd tried to join the Snake Charmers at her last school. She'd admired the way they hissed when greeting each other, and drew long coloured snakes up their bare arms in summer. They'd blindfolded her and told her to kneel on the grass with her mouth open. She'd known something nasty would be put into it, but she hadn't expected a live worm.

'You've failed,' they told her when she spat it out. 'You're supposed to keep it in your mouth while we count up to ten. You must do it again.'

'No way,' she'd said, and gone off and joined the Codemakers instead.

'There's not going to be worms, are there?' she asked now.

'Of course not,' Lindy said. 'Stand still.'

They were in a small side street that Anna did not recognise, standing near a corner. The sun had found a small gap in the clouds and shone down on dusty leaves and bright windows.

'Shut your eyes,' Lindy said.

Anna shut them. She felt a cloth put across them

and tied at the back of her head. Tied very tightly. Then two soft pads were slipped between the blindfold and her eyelids, making the darkness complete. Her world had vanished. She might have been standing in the very middle of nowhere.

'Lindy?' she asked nervously. 'Lindy, you haven't gone, have you?'

In answer, two thin hands grasped her shoulders and began to twirl her round until she felt giddy and was afraid she was going to fall.

'Hey!' she cried.

The hands steadied her.

'I'm taking you to the Hall of Secrets,' Lindy said, trying unsuccessfully to disguise her voice. 'Don't speak unless you're spoken to. Don't give the wrong answers or you'll be turned away.'

She began dragging Anna along by the arm, pushing her round a corner and on and on. The pavement seemed suddenly to tilt and tip, and Anna kept imagining brick walls a few centimetres from her nose. She was tempted to tear off the blindfold and say she didn't want to play. Pride prevented her.

At last they stopped. She heard the sound of a door opening.

'I don't know what I'm supposed to do,' she said, hanging back.

'I'm going to tell you, aren't I?' Lindy said. 'You didn't think I'd let my best friend make a muck of it, did you? Come on!'

Anna, pushed forward from behind, stumbled over a shallow step and nearly fell. She heard the door close behind them. She listened but could hear no other sound.

'We're in a passage,' Lindy whispered. 'In front of you is the door to the Hall of Secrets. Now I'm going to tell you exactly what to do and say. Listen carefully, Anna. You must remember. You must do it exactly right, or you'll get us both into trouble. Bad trouble. It's not a game, you know. It could be dangerous.'

3

Anna stood alone in front of the unseen door, holding in her hands the rod she had been given. She counted up to ten as she'd been instructed, and then knocked three times with the rod on the floor.

'The floor, mind, Anna, not the door. It's very important,' Lindy had said.

Anna waited. Silence. No sound of footsteps. No sound of a door opening. What was she supposed to do now? 'Knock only three times,' Lindy had said. 'Not more. Remember that, Anna.' But supposing nobody came?

Out of the silence, a voice said suddenly, so close to her that she fancied she felt the breath of it on her cheeks.

'Who is that knocking?'

It was a high, nasal voice, that half-sung the words like a choirboy. Anna was so startled that she forgot for a moment what she'd been told to say. There was a pause in which she heard invisible feet shuffle.

'A beggar,' she said, remembering at last.

'Where is your begging bowl?'

'In my heart and in my head.'

'Is it full or empty?'

'Empty.'

'Come in, then, beggar.'

Hands, not Lindy's for they were rougher and less thin, pulled her over the doorsill and dragged her forward.

'Kneel down,' a different voice said. 'You are in the presence of the secret lords of the Som – ' There was a muttered interruption, and the speaker added wearily, ' – and the Silver Lady, of course.'

The Silver Lady, Anna thought, as she knelt down obediently, that was Lindy. She felt better. The darkness of her blindfolded eyes, the strange voices and the feeling of unseen creatures all around her, smelling of sweat and dust, chewing-gum and candle-smoke, had begun to get her down. But it was only Lindy and her friends playing games. She had just to put up with the next few minutes; some silly tricks, cold water poured over her, spiders down her neck, mustard in her mouth. It wouldn't be anything terrible. They didn't murder new girls, did they?

'What do you want, beggar?' a third voice said.

To go home, Anna thought, but she didn't say it aloud. Instead, she said meekly, 'The gold of true companionship.'

'What will you give us in return?'

'The silver of secrecy.'

'Good. What else?'

'The. . . . The. . . .' She had forgotten. Lindy would be furious. Was furious. A thin finger, sharp as bone, poked her in the back. An angry whisper hissed in her ear, 'The blood of obedience.'

'The blood of obedience,' Anna repeated gratefully.

17

There was a pause. Then the speaker said, 'Did I hear someone prompting the applicant?'

'No.' This was Lindy's voice. 'I was just clearing my throat.'

Someone said, 'It doesn't matter, does it? Why don't we get on with it,' and someone else said, 'It's got to be done properly. We must have her blood first. Then the oath.'

My blood? thought Anna. Oh no, you don't.

Someone took hold of her hand and she tried to pull it away. A boy's voice said comfortingly, 'It won't hurt. And I've sterilised the needle in the candle flame, so it won't poison you. Be a brave bunny rabbit.'

'Ow!' Anna cried.

'There. All done. Now I'll just squeeze your finger. . . . That's it.'

'What are you going to do with my blood?' Anna asked suspiciously.

'I'm going to give it to my pet vampire to drink,' he whispered back, laughing, and she heard him move away.

They were muttering together now. She couldn't hear what they said. Her legs hurt. The floor was hard and gritty. When at last she was allowed to stand, she'd have a pattern of little red dents on her knees that would last for days.

'Can I get up?' she asked.

'No!' several voices chorussed. 'You haven't taken the oath yet. You're not a companion of the Som until you take the oath.'

18

'Can't I take it now?' Anna asked plaintively. 'My knees hurt.'

'You're not supposed to speak until you're spoken to!' Lindy said furiously. 'You've forgotten everything I told you. You must never complain. Never. You're supposed to be brave.'

There was a murmur of voices, all suggesting different things. That Anna should be made to kneel for another hour in penance. That she shouldn't be allowed to join – there should be no girls at all. That they should get the oath over with and get on with the feasting.

'Silence!' a voice said.

It was a deep voice, full of power. Immediately the talking stopped and there was silence, except for one voice, young and shrill, which said unnecessarily, 'Silence for the Goldmaster of the Som!'

'Thank you. Anna Cotman, are you willing to take the solemn oath?'

'Yes.'

'Say "Yes, Goldmaster," when you're addressing me.'

'Yes, Goldmaster.'

'That's better. Take off her blindfold.'

The tight cloth was pulled off roughly, taking one or two of her hairs with it. The pads of cotton wool fell to the ground. Anna blinked in the candle-light.

She was in a long, narrow room. The floor was of concrete and very dirty. The windows were covered with rough wooden shutters and only a very little light came through chinks here and there. There were

19

two long worktables, on which were placed several candles in jam jars.

In the flickering light, she saw six masked figures, and countless leaping shadows on the walls and on the floor. She was suddenly afraid. They're only boys behind those masks, she told herself. But they were bigger than she'd expected, and sat so still and silent while the shadows danced around them. Her heart beat faster.

'Look at me,' the deep voice commanded.

It was the one wearing the golden mask who spoke. He was tall. Some sort of purple cloth or cloak hid his clothes so that his body seemed to merge with the shadows. In contrast, his face shone. A ray of light from a crack in the wooden shutters fell on his bright hair and gleaming face, turning him into a golden idol.

Anna stared at him, half mesmerized. She thought he was beautiful. He reminded her of pictures in an old book on high chivalry, pictures of a young king with his knights around him, of heralds in bright colours lifting their bugles on high, and flags fluttering like candle flames in the wind.

'The swearing will begin,' he said. 'Anna Cotman, repeat after me – I wish to become a member of the Society of Masks.'

'I wish to become a member of the Society of Masks.'

'I promise to obey its rules or accept the punishment allotted to me.'

'I promise to obey its rules or accept the punishment allotted to me.'

20

'I take the solemn oath of secrecy.'

'I take the solemn oath of secrecy.'

'The Society of Masks is too secret to be called by name. From now on, I will never use this name but only call it the Som.'

'From now on . . . um . . . it's too secret . . .'

'Try to remember the words,' the Goldmaster said patiently.

'Sorry. Um . . . the Society of Masks . . . um – '

'Never mind. If you can't, you can't. Just say – I will only call it the Som.'

'I will only call it the Som,' Anna gabbled.

'Now concentrate, Anna Cotman. This part you must get right or you'll be thrown out. Do you understand?'

'Yes, Goldmaster.'

Five minutes ago, she wouldn't have minded at all being thrown out of this dark room into the daylight outside. But that was before she had seen the Goldmaster. Now she only thought of pleasing him.

'Repeat after me – ' he said. 'If I break this oath of secrecy, may the mask of bone break through my rotting flesh, may spiders build their webs in my eyes and worms feed on my brain.'

Anna repeated the words, concentrating so hard on remembering them correctly that she did not take in their meaning. Only much later, waking up in the middle of the night, did she think of them and feel uneasy.

The Goldmaster leaned forwards and dipped his finger into a small bowl that a boy in a green mask

21

was holding up to him. Then he traced the initials S O M on to her forehead with a red, wet fingertip.

'Now you are a companion of the Som,' he said. 'Our first companion for we are the lords, having been in it from the beginning. Oh, and the Silver Lady, of course. Companion, I name you . . . oh, the Silver Bird. Have you any money? It's a rule that a new companion has to buy coke and crisps for the rest of us. Silver Lady, go with her and see that she doesn't get lost.'

'But – but I – ' Anna stammered.

'Come on,' Lindy said, pushing her towards the door, 'and shut up.'

'I haven't enough money,' Anna whispered, hot with embarrassment.

'I have. I'll lend you some.'

When the girls had gone, the boys began taking off their masks and folding up the coloured sheets they had used as cloaks to hide their ordinary clothes.

'Poor little rabbit,' Tom Smith said. 'I think she was scared.'

'Not nearly scared enough,' a fat, baby-faced boy said. 'We ought to make the oath more horrible.'

There was a murmur of agreement, and they turned to look at the Goldmaster. He alone had not yet removed his mask. Holding a broken piece of mirror in his hand, he stood admiring his golden face in the candle-light.

'She was very eager to please, wasn't she?' he asked, the satisfaction in his voice making it obvious he took the credit for this. 'Quite effective, this mask, isn't it? You'd never know it was me, would you?'

'I'd know you anywhere, Jeremy,' Tom Smith said, laughing. 'No one else is so fond of mirrors. But it might fool other people. Silly little girls, especially. Don't tease her too much. She reminds me of a pet rabbit I once had.'

'What happened to it?'

'Somebody let it out of its hutch. It ran away and we never saw it again.'

'I wonder who had rabbit pie that night,' the fat boy said.

Jeremy laughed, and turned his golden face back to the mirror.

4

The Hall of Secrets, seen from the outside, turned out to be a small one-storey building, squeezed in between a second-hand furniture shop and a builder's merchants. A sign over its door said: W.H. BRIGGS & SON. Party Novelties. Jokes. Paper Masks.

'We found a whole box of masks in there,' Lindy said, seeing Anna look up at the sign. 'A lot of them were stained – with damp, not blood or anything interesting – but the others were all right. I bagged the best one. I painted it silver myself.' She stopped as if for applause, but Anna was brushing the grit off her knees and didn't say anything. 'You'll have to have a mask too,' Lindy went on. 'I'm afraid yours can't be silver. I mean, *I* wouldn't mind, but I don't think the boys would agree. After all, you're only an ordinary member, just a companion, so you can't expect to be silver like me, can you?'

'I don't mind,' Anna said. 'Except – well, the Goldmaster said I was to be called the Silver Bird, so I thought – '

'Oh, Jeremy always gets things wrong.'

'Jeremy?'

'Jeremy. You know, my brother. You are funny.

Didn't you know the Goldmaster was my brother. You don't know anything, do you?' Lindy said, with a little squeal of laughter, though why she should find it so funny, Anna had no idea. How was she supposed to know? Nobody had told her.

She felt oddly let down. The boy with his golden face had seemed magical. She didn't want him to be anybody's brother. Brothers were commonplace. Lots of people had them and complained that they were noisy and greedy and didn't wash their feet often enough.

Lindy did not exactly say this, but nevertheless with every word she spoke, the image of the shining boy began to tarnish.

'Of course, *he* wouldn't have one of the ordinary masks. They weren't good enough for him. He's awfully vain, you know. He went up to town to one of those theatrical shops for his. I bet it cost the earth. Not that that would worry him. It's only Harry's money.'

'Who's Harry?' Anna asked, half-expecting to be laughed at again for not knowing. But Lindy was eager to tell her.

'He's our stepfather,' she said. 'We refuse to call him Dad. We hate him. It's great fun. He's a property developer and has bags of money, and he's always trying to bribe us. You know, buy our love. That's what Jeremy says. We take his presents and thank him coldly – as if we didn't really want them but were too polite to say so. We don't even smile. Mum gets wild, but we tell her you can't love to order. I mean, nobody could love Harry King. He's a horrid little man. He wears a gold tie-pin. Everybody in Redmarsh hates him.'

'Because he wears a gold tie-pin?' Anna asked, puzzled, for what was wrong with that?

Lindy squealed with laughter again. Anna, flushing, smiled quickly, pretending she'd meant to be funny.

'Because he's a property developer,' Lindy said. 'They're afraid he's going to put up office blocks all over the place and spoil their view of the river. They talk like he's a shark come to gobble us up. He has got a shark's eyes, come to think of it. Small and cold. You wait till you see him. You'll hate him, too.'

Anna was silent. You can't hate to order, either. She felt sorry for Harry King whom nobody loved. Except –

'Your mother must love him,' she said. 'She married him.'

Lindy shrugged. 'He's rich.' Seeing Anna looked shocked, she added, 'I suppose you think I'm awful.'

'No,' Anna said doubtfully.

'His latest bribe is saying we can have the old workshop. You know, the Hall of Secrets,' Lindy said with a sly smile.

'Has he really given it to you?' Anna asked, impressed.

'Well, not given exactly. But he told Jeremy that he and his friends could use it and gave him the keys. He meant it for me, too, whatever Jeremy says. I bet he hopes we'll make so much noise that we'll drive the old woman out.'

'What old woman?'

'The one in the junk shop next door. He wants the

26

land and she won't sell. I told Jeremy we must be as quiet as mice. Then we found the box of masks and somebody said we should be a secret society. Not kid's stuff. A proper one, like the Freemasons. You know, with rules and rituals, where you all have to swear to be faithful and come to each other's aid, come what may. Tom Smith said it would help us deal with the bully gangs at school. He said if there were enough of us, they'd leave us alone. But he didn't want it to be secret.'

'Why not?'

'He said nasty things breed under stones. He's always making silly remarks like that. He's a pain in the neck. I can't think why Jeremy likes him.'

'Which one is he?'

'He's the one in the green mask. You'll see when we get back.'

But when they got back to the workshop, they found the outer door was locked against them. Anna put the heavy carrier bag down on the pavement and eased her cramped fingers, while Lindy knocked.

Then, hardly giving anyone time to answer, Lindy suddenly lost her temper and began hammering with both fists on the door.

'Beasts! Beasts!' she cried shrilly. 'Filthy beasts!'

Anna watched her in astonishment.

'Lindy, what's the matter?' she asked.

'They've locked us out, that's what's the matter. I should've known. You don't think they wanted us, do you? God, you're green! I had to threaten to tell Harry if they refused to let me join. And they certainly didn't want *you*. I'll show them!'

She looked round wildly for some sort of weapon with which to beat the door down. Finding nothing suitable, she kicked it viciously; then started hopping on one foot and howling.

'Oh! Oh God! I've broken my foot! I can't bear it! Anna, *do something!*'

'Do what?' Anna asked helplessly, for when she tried to support Lindy, Lindy screeched and hopped away from her, flapping her arms like a demented hen.

'Send for an ambulance. Quick, Anna!'

Before Anna could move, the door opened. A fat boy in blue demins and a red mask stood in the doorway.

'What's going on here?' he asked, in the same nasal, high-pitched voice Anna had heard earlier.

'We've got to ring for an ambulance. Lindy's broken her foot,' she cried.

'Oh, don't be so silly,' Lindy said, pushing past her. 'Of course I haven't. I just stubbed my toe. Why was the door locked, Red Lord?'

'To give us time to put our masks on again,' he said. 'It was the Goldmaster's idea. He said *she* shouldn't be allowed to see our faces. And she's not to know our outside names either. She's only a companion. She's not one of us.'

'That's not fair,' Anna said indignantly. 'I've taken the oath. And anyway I know who – '

'She knows who I am,' Lindy interrupted quickly, with an imploring look. A look that said plainly – "Don't tell them I told you who the Goldmaster is.

Remember I'm your very best friend. Don't give me away."

So Anna kept quiet and followed them into the hall.

The masked figures sat in a semi-circle on the floor. There were the same flickering candles, the same leaping shadows. There was the Goldmaster wrapped in his purple cloak, his golden face shining like the sun. But the magic had gone.

He was only Jeremy Miller who was vain and hated his stepfather. The Green Lord, sitting next to him, was Tom Smith who didn't like secrets. Silver Lady, just putting her mask on again, was Lindy. The Red Lord was fat and had a high, nasal voice. That only left two, the Blue Lord and the White Lord. She looked at them very carefully.

I'll know them again, she thought, by the shape of their heads and hands, by the sound of their voices, by the way they move. I'll know them again, the secret lords of the Som.

The Silver Lady was whispering to the Goldmaster. He listened for a moment, then nodded.

'Companion,' he said, turning his beautiful, shining face towards Anna, 'I re-name you Yellow Bird. You can't be silver. You're not a lady of the Som. Now hand out the coke and crisps.' Anna did not move. 'Remember your vow of obedience,' he said sharply.

Silently she handed out the tins of coke and bags of crisps and biscuits.

Nobody thanked her. Taking her own, she went a little way off and sat on the floor, facing them. Watching them.

Six masked faces. Gold and silver, red and green, blue and white. Six full masks that covered all the face, leaving only the holes through which their eyes glittered in the candle-light. Idiots. Anna smiled to herself. She opened her bag of crisps and began to eat noisily and with relish.

It was Green Mask who laughed.

'Hey, she's got us,' he said. 'How can we eat with these things on? I don't know about you lot, but I'm hungry.' He took his mask off, revealing a very ordinary face, with mouse-brown hair and no distinguishing features. 'You won't remember me, will you, bunny rabbit?' he said. 'Nobody ever does. I've got an instantly forgettable face. Teachers are always calling me by other boy's names. Even my mother once kissed the wrong boy. I'm safe enough.'

The others looked towards the Goldmaster, waiting for a lead. He was silent for a moment. Then he said, 'Yellow Bird, you are excused. You may go.'

'I haven't finished my coke and crisps yet,' she protested.

'Go!' he said coldly. 'You must learn not to question our orders. Remember you have taken the oath. It's too late to back out now.'

'Do you want to die?' the Red Lord asked, leaning forwards. 'Do you want to die horribly. Remember the words?' He began to chant in his high-pitched, sing-song voice, 'If I break this oath, may the mask of bone break through my rotting flesh, may spiders build their webs in my eyes and worms feed on my brain.'

'I didn't mean it!'

30

'Then you shouldn't have said it.'

'Go now,' the Goldmaster said.

The candle flames ducked and then grew tall. The shadows of the masked lords leaped up to the ceiling. She hated the way their eyes moved behind their blank paper faces. The Silver Lady kept quiet.

They were bigger than she was, and older. There were six of them and only one of her. She was in a strange room in a strange part of the city and she was frightened. Despising herself, she got to her feet and left the building.

'Did you have a nice afternoon, love?' her grandmother asked her over supper.

Anna wanted to say that she'd had a horrid afternoon. That she didn't want to be a companion of the Som. She didn't want to be the very best friend of Lindy Miller. She hated Redmarsh and her new school, and she wished they could go back to Muswell Hill where she'd been happy. But her grandmother had put all her savings into the wool shop. She was old and had high blood pressure and worrying was bad for her. But it was more than that. Anna knew she was afraid to break the terrible oath of secrecy she had taken.

So she smiled and said, 'Yeah, Gran. Super.'

5

On Sunday morning, Mrs Cotman took Anna to church.

'It'll give us a chance to meet people,' she said.

Like Anna, she did not feel at home yet in Redmarsh. The small flat above the wool shop kept knocking their elbows with unexpected corners; the people in the streets didn't smile at them; the marshy river gave even the air they breathed an unfamiliar taste.

'We'll have a word with the vicar,' she said. 'There may be something we can join.'

'No!' Anna said.

Her grandmother looked at her curiously, and Anna gave a nervous smile. 'You said yourself we shouldn't rush into things – you know, commit ourselves.'

Mrs Cotman laughed. 'I was only thinking of a sewing group. Or perhaps yoga classes. I wasn't proposing to sign my soul away – Anna, why are you looking like that? What's the matter?'

'Nothing.'

'You had a nightmare last night. The first in years. Did anything happen to upset you yesterday?'

Anna shook her head. She had dreamed that she was surrounded by a ring of candle flames, and through their smoke she had seen cloaked figures dancing. The candles had dipped and then burned tall and clear. She'd seen the dancers' terrible grinning faces, masks of bone, skulls. She'd heard her own voice repeating the dreadful oath, and the sound of laughter. . . .

'I expect it was only the prawns we had for tea,' she said.

'They tasted all right to me,' her grandmother told her.

St Peter's Church was only three streets away. They arrived early and sat near the back so that they could watch the people coming in. The fine weather kept the congregation small. Anna, making a selection of possible friends for her grandmother, found her choice restricted. It was like choosing chocolates from a half-empty box. Not that one, looks hard-centred. And that one's just a jelly. That one's too small. Why, it's Lindy!

Lindy Miller minced along the aisle, wearing a bright pink dress and a virtuous expression, neither of which particularly suited her. She was with a fair, fancy-looking woman, and a short, stocky man with steel-rimmed spectacles. Must be her mother and the hated stepfather, Harry King.

A boy was walking behind them. He was tall and his hair shone like polished brass. As he moved forward, light from a stained-glass window patterned his face with a mask of colour; crimson and gold, green and blue.

The Goldmaster. She had heard his voice in her dream, 'Repeat the solemn words after me. . . .'

Please, I didn't mean them. I was only funning. He isn't anything special. He's only Lindy's older brother, Jeremy – and he's got a spot on the back of his neck!

The four of them had walked past her and her grandmother without a glance and now sat in the pew in front of them. Lindy can't have seen me, Anna thought, or she'd turn round and smile. She's so near. If her hair were shorter, she'd feel my breath on the back of her neck.

She leaned forward and blew as hard as she could, hoping to part Lindy's lank hair and reach her bare skin. All she got for this was her grandmother's elbow in her ribs.

She waited until the first hymn: her favourite, 'To be a Pilgrim'. Leaning forward, she sang directly into Lindy's right ear, substituting her own words for the proper ones –

'Lindy Miller, look at me,
Turn your eyes hither.
Here is one who'll constant be,
Come wind, come weather . . .'

She stopped sheepishly when her grandmother pinched her arm. Harry King turned his head. With his sallow face and the light shining on his round spectacles, he looked like some blind night creature. To her surprise, he smiled at her.

When the hymn came to an end, he bent down and whispered something to Lindy. Lindy shook her head.

He told her I was trying to attract her attention,

34

Anna thought. Why did she shake her head? Why won't she look round? Doesn't she want to be my friend any more?

I don't care!

She tried to concentrate on the service, but her eyes kept going to the brother and sister in front of her. When it was over, she stood up and waited for them to leave their pew. Harry King nodded and smiled at her. The other three walked past as if she did not exist. Jeremy's glance skimmed over her blankly. She might've been part of the wall, and a dull part, too. Lindy looked straight ahead as if she were wearing blinkers.

'Lindy – ' Anna said.

'Can't stop,' Lindy whispered, stopping nonetheless. 'Got to go out with Beauty and the Beast. That's what we call them.' She nodded towards her mother and stepfather who had gone on ahead. 'Good, isn't it? Where's Jeremy? Oh, he's gone.'

'When will I see – '

'It's all in there,' Lindy said, pushing a note into her hand. Then she ran off.

They followed slowly. Mrs Cotman stopped in the porch to talk to the vicar and Anna walked out into the sunlight. Sitting down on a low grass mound, she looked at the piece of paper in her hand, on which was written:

YAVE GITH AARRY LEE
HO WUM HACK SOU
TO MND BATE YMONDA

After a moment she screwed it up in her hand and looked for somewhere to throw it.

'Give it to me,' a voice said.

She looked up and saw a boy. He was a year or two older than she was, and had mouse-coloured hair and unremarkable features. A very ordinary-looking boy. She smiled.

'I remember you,' she said.

'You're not supposed to,' he told her. 'I look like too many other boys. Are you sure you're not thinking of one at your last school?'

'I never think of them. They used to pull my hair and put worms in my mouth.'

'Just high spirits,' Tom Smith said. 'Harmless. Better than – '

'Than what?'

'Oh, I dunno,' he said, shrugging. 'Do you want me to translate that note for you?'

'No, thanks. I've already done it.'

He stared at her. 'I don't believe you,' he said, sounding hurt. 'It's in a double code. I made it up myself.' He smoothed out the crumpled paper. 'What does it say, then, if you're so clever.'

'Have to go with Mum and Harry. Back late. See you Monday,' Anna said.

'Lindy must've told you.'

'She didn't. I worked it out. It's easy. You read it downwards, not across. Then you put the first letter of each word at the beginning of the next word all the time, until the last word when you take the last letter and – '

'All right, you're a genius,' he said, in tones of great disgust.

'I belonged to a club called the Codemakers at my

last school,' she explained. 'We were always making up codes and solving other people's. It's just practice, that's all.'

'I forgive you,' he said, smiling. 'Perhaps you can help us make up a better one. That is – ' He hesitated and glanced round the churchyard to see if there was anyone in earshot. Most of the people had already gone. Mrs Cotman was still with the vicar who was writing something on a piece of paper. Tom said in a low voice, 'Are you sure you want to be a companion of the Som, Anna?'

'Yes, I suppose so. I mean I have to be. I've already taken the oath,' she said in confusion, for he sounded so serious. 'Why shouldn't I? Is there anything wrong with it?'

'Perhaps not. Though – take my advice and play with kids your own age.'

'I'm as old as Lindy!' Anna said indignantly.

'Oh, Lindy was born old. She can take care of herself. She's a proper little – ' He broke off, looking over her shoulder. She turned and saw with surprise that Jeremy Miller had come back and was walking towards them.

'Don't say it, Tom,' he advised. 'I know your opinion of Lindy, but she is my sister, after all. I might feel I ought to knock you down, or something boring like that.' He looked at Anna, his eyes as blue and blank as if he'd never seen her before. 'Is this Lindy's new friend?' he asked. 'Well, well, they get smaller every time. Tell me, will you really be constant, come wind, come weather?'

He'd heard her singing. Anna flushed hotly and mumbled, 'Yes.'

He smiled at her. 'Good. I admire loyalty. Lindy hasn't been lucky with her friends. And you needn't snigger, Tom. I know what you think and you're being unfair.'

'I think rabbits should be warned against snakes in the grass. Don't you, Anna?'

Anna, who had been staring at Jeremy, looked confused.

'Grass snakes aren't poisonous,' she said, puzzled.

The boys laughed and walked away together.

6

'You don't want to talk to *them*,' Lindy said, linking her arm through Anna's and drawing her away from the other girls in the playground. 'They're terribly nosy,' she went on loudly, before they were decently out of earshot. 'You've got to watch what you say. You don't want to break your oath, do you?'

'They were only asking about our maths homework.'

'Cunning devils. They get you talking about algebra to put you off your guard, and the next thing you know is you've told all. Haven't you seen old war films on telly? You're not supposed to tell the enemy anything. Don't show them photos of your gran or tell them the name of your hamster or what you had for breakfast. Once you start talking, it's like running down a steep hill, you can't stop. Didn't you know that? You don't know anything, do you, Anna? It's a good thing you've got me to look after you.'

Anna sighed. She'd been friends with Lindy for several weeks now and found it a lonely honour. Lindy had no other friends and saw to it that Anna could not make any. Every time she saw anyone talking to Anna, she came rushing up like an officious sheepdog and snapped them away. At times, Anna thought longingly of her old school. Nobody had bossed her about there. She'd been important in Muswell Hill. Admired.

Here she was a nobody. The lords of the Som called her a companion but treated her like a slave. 'Fetch this. Carry that. Pick up those tins, wash those mugs, clear up that mess.' She wasn't allowed to attend the meetings of the inner council nor see their faces nor know their real names –

Ha! She'd been too clever for them there. Anna smiled.

'What are you smirking at?' Lindy asked.

'People are funny,' Anna told her. 'They think they've only got to hide their faces and you won't know them. They forget they've got hands and feet and voices.'

'What do you mean?'

'I know their names,' Anna said with simple pride. 'I know them all, the secret lords of the Som. The Red Lord is Duncan Stretton, the Blue Lord Ali Patel and –'

'Shut up!' Lindy cried. 'Are you mad?' She looked anxiously around but nobody was paying them any attention. 'Don't ever do that again. I suppose Tom Smith told you.'

'Nobody told me. I found out for myself,' Anna said, wanting to tell Lindy all about it, how she'd studied the masked lords, noticing an inkstain on a shoe, a scar on an arm, a bandaged finger – and found them again in the school playground on second and third form boys, walking around carelessly and

40

thinking themselves unsuspected. Calling each other openly by their real names and never guessing that a small, despised first-former was taking it all in.

But Lindy didn't want to hear how clever Anna had been. She interrupted her ruthlessly, her shrill voice drowning out Anna's.

'It must've been Tom. You're very thick with him.'

'I've been helping him with the new code – '

'So that's your doing. I might've guessed. It's stupid, Anna. All those Zs and Xs everywhere, nobody could understand it. It's worse than maths.'

'You're not supposed to understand it without the key,' Anna retorted, stung, for she'd been proud of the new code. 'It's not my fault you keep losing it. Tom thought it was very clever.'

Lindy was silent for a moment, looking cross. Then she said, with a note of satisfaction in her voice, 'I suppose you know he's leaving at the end of the term?'

'What?'

'His dad's being sent to France for a year by his firm and he's taking Tom with him. He'll be going to an international school in Paris. Didn't he tell you?'

'No.'

Anna felt depressed. Tom Smith was in the third form at school so she hardly ever saw him, except from a distance. But in the Hall of Secrets, he had often stood her friend, stopping the other lords from teasing her too unkindly, helping her carry anything he thought too heavy for her and once even telling Lindy off for being too bossy. And now he was going. Anna sighed.

'Just look at your face!' Lindy jeered. 'I do believe you're going to cry. Want to borrow my hanky?'

'Don't be stupid!'

Lindy laughed and began prancing around her, waving her hanky in the air like a Morris dancer. 'Wait till I tell Tom. Poor Anna. Shall I ask him to kiss you goodbye?'

People were looking at them now. Anna felt her cheeks burn.

'Leave me alone!' she cried furiously. 'I hate you!'

Lindy stopped dancing. Her face seemed to shrink. A look of intense concentration came over it, and after a moment, tears filled her eyes and ran silently down her cheeks. She made no attempt to hide them but just stood there like a dripping tap.

'Nobody likes me,' she said. 'Nobody at all. Not even my own mother.'

'Of course she does,' Anna assured her, though she wasn't at all sure that this was true. Mrs King was as pretty as a painted lily, but cold. It seemed to Anna that she loved only herself. Even as she spoke to you, her eyes would slide away to the mirror on the wall. Sometimes, when she looked at Jeremy, she smiled, as if seeing her own reflection in his face. But for poor Lindy, she had mostly frowns –

'Please stop pulling those faces when you talk, Lindy. When did you wash your hair last? It looks terrible . . .'

Her husband she usually ignored. He sat at the head of the table and might have been a chair for all the notice she took of him. Meal times were silent. Jeremy ate rapidly and left the table before anyone

42

else had finished. Even Lindy seemed subdued. Harry King did his best but nobody helped. His remarks seemed to hang in the air, unclaimed, until Anna, sorry for him, agreed timidly that yes, it was a beautiful day, or no, she hadn't heard Mr Tebbit's attack on the media.

'He wasn't talking to you, silly,' Lindy said later. 'He was talking to Mum.'

'Then why didn't she answer him?' Anna asked.

'She finds us boring,' Lindy had said. 'Me and old moneybags both. I don't care.'

But she did care, of course. Those tears must be real, Anna thought, even if it did look as though she'd squeezed them out of her eyes. There'd been a girl at Anna's last school who could cry on purpose. 'It's easy,' she'd said. 'I just have to think of something sad.' Poor Lindy. 'Nobody likes me,' she'd said. 'Not even my own mother' – that was sad enough, wasn't it?

So when Lindy said mournfully, 'And now you don't want to be my friend any more,' Anna said that of course she did.

'Promise? Promise you'll be my friend for ever?'

Forever is a long time. But Anna remembered Jeremy smiling down at her in the sunlight and saying, 'Will you really be constant, come wind, come weather?'

'All right, I promise,' she said.

Lindy's tears stopped immediately and a satisfied smile took their place.

Mrs Cotman was right. Anna was too soft. Any thin, unhappy neighbourhood cat could catch her.

* * *

'I'm not a boy given to gloomy premonitions and stuff like that,' Tom Smith said, a week or two before the end of term, 'but if I were you, I'd get out of here and never come back.'

He and Anna were sitting at one of the tables in the Hall of Secrets, painting paper masks for the new companions who were to be sworn in next week. They were alone. Lindy was having her piano lesson and the others had not turned up. It was a hot bright evening, and they preferred to be out and about, rather than sitting in the dim, stuffy workroom, painting masks. Let Anna do it. That's what she was there for. And Tom Smith, if he wanted to be a fool.

'Why are you always warning me against the Som?' Anna asked. 'You never warn Lindy.'

'I never dream about Lindy. Thank God.'

She stared at him. 'You mean you do dream about me?'

'You needn't look so pleased. It's not by choice, I assure you,' he said. 'I'd rather dream about Daisy Appleford in 5A. Much rather. Now she's got a complexion like a ripe peach. And a figure – wow!'

Anna ignored this. She was fascinated by the thought of shadowy Annas, living secret lives in other people's dreams. What had Tom's Anna been like? And Gran's? And Lindy's? She wondered if they would recognise each other if they met in the street.

'What was I doing in your dream?' she asked curiously.

'You were screaming,' he said.

'*Screaming*?'

He nodded. 'Your face was as white as this,' he

said, picking up an unpainted mask. 'You were standing over there, backed up against the wall. There were other people in the room, a crowd of them. Hooded. Masked. They were chanting something. I couldn't make out the words. You were screaming too loudly.'

'*Why*?'

'How should I know? You were doing the screaming, not me.'

'It was your dream.'

'Yes, it was. And I'll thank you to keep out of my dreams in future, Anna Cotman.'

She smiled uncertainly, not knowing if he was teasing her or not. Lindy was always telling her she was too gullible. 'You didn't believe *that*?' she'd say, shrieking with laughter. 'You are daft. Anyone could take you in. You're so wet behind the ears, it's a wonder your head doesn't shrink.'

Anna sighed. She looked at Tom. He was concentrating on the mask he was painting, whistling soundlessly. He looked cheerful, not at all like someone who had dark forebodings. Well, why should he worry? He wouldn't be here much longer. He was going off to France for a year. Perhaps his dad would decide to stay out there for good, and she'd never see Tom again. There was already a new lord of the Som, who'd been sworn in two days ago, in a secret ceremony Anna had not been allowed to attend.

'Who's the new lord, Tom?'

'You know you're not supposed to ask me that,' he said.

'Stupid rules,' she muttered.

He laughed. 'Better not say that to the new lord or he'll thump you. Stay away from him, he looks fierce. I don't know who he is. I'd tell you if I did. He was all dressed up from head to foot in yellow, like a Chinese funeral.'

'Why didn't you ask him his name?'

'I did. He said, "I'm the Lord of the Yellow." Pompous ass! I said I meant his real name and he said that was his proper name in here. "If we ever meet outside," he said, "you can ask me my name again, but I doubt if we will. I hear you're leaving us soon." – making me sound like a deserter. The Goldmaster laughed and they walked off together. You know who the Goldmaster is, don't you?' Tom asked, obviously willing to tell her if she didn't. His loyalty to the Som, she suspected, had never been very great. He was the boy who didn't like secrets.

'Yes, it's Jeremy. Lindy's brother,' she said.

'And he can be a stupid clot at times,' Tom muttered.

'I thought he was your best friend,' Anna said, shocked.

'Best? I dunno. I don't go setting my friends exams and awarding them points. Jeremy's OK, even if he can't see further than the end of his nose. Now you're looking disapproving.'

'I think one should be loyal to one's friends,' Anna said primly.

He smiled and shook his head. 'My poor bunny rabbit,' he said. 'You should've been more careful choosing your friends. Loyalty will get you into a nasty mess one of these days, if you don't look out.'

7

It was the first week of the summer holidays. Anna and Lindy were sitting in the long grass at the edge of the common. In front of them a small boy threw sticks for a black and white spaniel. Two joggers with red faces went puffing past. It was very hot.

Anna didn't want to go to the gloomy workshop, smelling of dirt and damp and wet cardboard.

'Do we have to? It's so stuffy in there,' she complained. 'We can't even open the windows because they insist on keeping them boarded up. Let's go swimming instead. They won't miss us.'

'That's just it,' Lindy said. 'That's the whole point. They've been trying to edge us out for weeks. Now Tom's gone, we've got no one to stick up for us. If we're not careful, we'll find ourselves out in the cold.'

The cold, Anna thought wistfully, lying back and gazing up at the hot blue sky. 'Would that matter?' she asked.

'It would matter to me,' Lindy said stiffly. 'Why should Jeremy always have everything? I won't let them push me out. You go swimming if you want. I'll go there alone.' She stood up, very straight, like a martyr tied to a stake. 'Don't worry about me,' she said, her eyes filling with tears.

Anna sighed. 'Oh, all right, all right. I'll come.'

Lindy cheered up immediately, as she always did when she got her own way. She didn't even give her tears time to dry before she was smiling again. There should have been rainbows on her face.

'Are you looking forward to the swearing-in on Saturday?' she asked, as they walked off the common. 'I am. Remember when you were sworn in? The Red Lord says that was nothing. He says this one is going to be simply horrible. His dad's a butcher, and Red's going to sneak out a bucket of old bones and pig's liver and those nasty bits of insides.'

'What's he going to do with them?'

'He won't say. He just smirks. Something nasty, I bet. They'll be scared rigid. I wouldn't miss it for the world, would you?'

'No,' Anna said cheerfully.

She wasted no sympathy on the new companions. They were all going to be boys. They could look after themselves. Though she was glad she was no longer going to be the only companion, she had little hope that they would help her with the chores. The lords of the Som didn't seem to have heard of women's lib.

'It's not fair,' she said. 'Why aren't there any girls?'

'It's that new lord,' Lindy told her. 'I wanted to choose some girls but he said I couldn't. I hate him. He's put all the other lords against me. Not that that took much doing. But he's not going to get away with it. That's why I need you, Anna.'

'Me?' Anna asked nervously. 'What can I do?'

48

'You found out who the other lords were. I want you to help me find him out.'

'Don't you know who he is?'

'I've never seen him without his mask. Nobody has. At least, I suppose Jeremy must've done. He must know who he is, but he's not telling. I don't think that's right, do you?'

'No,' Anna said.

'Jeremy's changed. I used to be able to get my own way if I went on and on at him, and cried. He's very weak, you see. I could always get him to tell me things. But he won't now. He shouted at me. I thought he was going to hit me. I wish he had. I'd have told Harry. I'd have shown him the bruise.'

Anna was silent. She knew Lindy was jealous of her brother. She claimed she hated Harry, yet Anna had seen her watching him resentfully when he spoke to Jeremy, as if she were counting his words to see that her brother didn't get more than his fair share. Lindy wanted someone, even if it were only Harry, to love her best.

'Will you help me?' Lindy asked.

'I'll try. It's the hands — that's what gives them away. Scars, scratches, insect bites, the shape of their nails — '

'He wears gloves.'

'Gloves? In this weather?'

Lindy nodded. 'Yellow ones,' she said.

'Oh.'

'That's why I wanted us to be there early,' Lindy went on. 'Before he has time to disguise himself. He must come in the back way and change in the store-room, because the door suddenly opens and he's there. All dressed in yellow from head to foot like – '

'Like a banana?' Anna suggested, but Lindy did not laugh.

'I was going to try and catch him out by myself,' she said, as they walked down the pavement towards the old workshop, 'but I'm glad you're coming with me, Anna. I'm glad there're two of us. I'd have been a bit scared on my own. Silly, isn't it? But he's. . . . I don't know. He gives me the creeps.'

There was a small yard at the back of the old workshop, surrounded by a high brick wall. The double gates that led into it were locked. Anna tried to look disappointed. But Lindy had obviously expected this. She led Anna round to the front and opened the door with her key.

The bright daylight spilled in behind them.

'Shall I light the candles before you close the door?' Anna asked.

'No. There'll be light enough. Our eyes will soon get used to it. We don't want the others to know we're here early.'

The door closed and they stood in the dim passage, lit only by a dirty skylight. The workroom door was open, showing a darkness made more confusing by the bright chinks and cracks in the wooden shutters.

'Where now?' Anna asked.

'We'll have to go through the workroom to the store at the back. There's a way out into the yard from there. It's where they used to load the vans.'

They fumbled their way through the speckled dark, knocking themselves against the long tables and yelping. The storeroom door was locked.

Lindy swore. Shook the handle. Kicked the door.

'Isn't there another way?' Anna asked.

The workroom and the small office were at the front. Only the storeroom and the lavatory overlooked the yard at the back. The lavatory had a small window with opaque glass and cobwebs.

'It won't open,' Anna said.

'It's just stuck. Let me try.' Lindy pushed Anna out of the way and twisted the rusty metal handle with all her strength. It came off in her hands. Angrily she hit the glass with it. The window shattered.

Shards of glass fell down into the yard outside, letting in a burst of jagged sunlight.

'That's done it,' Lindy said and giggled. She began knocking out the remaining pieces of glass. Then she stopped abruptly, turned and pushed Anna out of the room, following her so quickly that she nearly knocked her over. She shut the door behind them and leant against it, her face white.

'What's the matter?'

'He's out there. In the yard.'

'Who? The new lord?'

Lindy nodded. She looked terrified.

'Did you see his face?'

'No. He's got his mask on. But he saw mine.' Lindy was nearly crying, real tears this time, Anna thought, astonished.

For a moment, Lindy's face infected her. She clutched Lindy's arm and stared up and down the

51

dim passage, wondering which way to run. But running wouldn't help. Besides, what had they done that was so terrible?

'It was only a small window,' she whispered. 'We could offer to pay for it. Gran would lend me some money.'

'Oh, Harry'll pay for it,' Lindy said, letting go of Anna's hand and drawing herself up. 'He won't mind. After all, we were only trying to open the window. It must've been cracked. The glass simply fell out, didn't it?'

'Yes,' Anna agreed. 'We didn't lay a finger on it.'

They smiled at each other. Then Lindy said boldly, 'Anyway, it's none of his business. He can't say anything to me. I'm the Silver Lady. I've got as much right here as he has. More, in fact – '

A sudden noise from the workroom made her jump and fall silent. Anna looked at her curiously. Then she heard footsteps, quick, light. The door opened.

A figure stood in the doorway, all in yellow; a dark yellow in the dim light, more mustard then lemon. The long yellow robe brushed the dirty floor, the yellow hood fell forward, shadowing the masked face, and the gloved hands were hidden in wide yellow sleeves. Except for a dark glitter of eyes behind the eyeholes, there was nothing showing of the person concealed within the yellow cloth, nothing for sharp eyes to note and remember.

'So it is the Silver Lady,' he said. 'I thought it was you I saw through the broken glass. Do tell me why you broke it. The window was filthy, it's true. But surely the companion could have cleaned it for you, if you wanted to see out?'

A posh voice, Tom had called it. Yes. Very self-assured. Sarcastic. It could've been a man speaking. Would she recognise the voice again? Anna wasn't sure. The mask distorted the sound.

Lindy had muttered some reply. Anna didn't hear what. Now the Yellow Lord was looking at her.

'Who are you? Why aren't you wearing your mask? Don't you know the rules?'

'We only just got here.'

'What's your name?'

'Anna. Anna Cotman.'

'Not that name,' Lindy said angrily. She had put on her silver mask in a hurry. It was crooked. She looked like a tipsy moon. 'I've told you. I've told you a hundred times. She's Yellow Bird. Birdie for short,' she added, turning to the hooded figure. 'She's a companion. The only one at the moment until the new ones are sworn in.'

'Yellow Bird,' he said, stressing the word 'yellow'. 'So you're one of mine, are you? Go and put on your mask and report back to me.'

He went back into the workroom, leaving the door open behind him. Anna watched him as he began lighting the candles and saw his hooded shadow spring up on the walls.

'Who does he think he is,' she muttered resentfully.

He must have had ears like a fox for he stopped immediately, and spun round on his heel so quickly that his yellow robe swirled out round his ankles like water. His shoes, showing briefly, were black and polished and narrow.

'I am the Lord of the Yellow,' he said. 'I wouldn't try and cross me, Birdie, I really wouldn't. Remember your oath.'

Then he walked away. His feet, now invisible again beneath his long robe, made a light slapping noise on the concrete floor. He went into the storeroom and shut the door behind him. They heard the sound of the key turning in the lock.

'That's it,' Anna said. 'That's done it. I'm going and I'm never coming back. Never.'

'Anna – '

'Don't try and stop me. It's all your fault, Lindy. I couldn't be Silver Bird, oh no! You wanted to be silver all by yourself, so I had to be plain yellow. And now that creature says I'm one of his. Like hell!'

'Anna – '

'It's no good crying at me, Lindy – '

'I wasn't going to cry,' Lindy said. She looked thoughtful for a moment, and then added very sweetly, 'I do think you're brave, Anna. I do really. I couldn't do it, not for a hundred pounds. I'd be too frightened.'

'What do you mean?' Anna asked suspiciously.

'He'll be wild if you don't report back. You're supposed to obey your lord, it's in the rules. If you don't go, it'll show him up in front of the other lords. He'll never forgive you. I know the type. He'll be out for your blood.'

'Don't be silly,' Anna said uneasily.

'The blood of obedience, that's what you swore to give, remember?'

'Load of rubbish,' Anna muttered, but she looked nervous.

'It's a pity we don't know his name,' Lindy said regretfully. 'I mean, if he murders you, I won't be able to tell the police who did it. He could just vanish.'

'Idiot!'

'But if you wait a day or two, I'll help you find out who he is. Then you'll be safe. He wouldn't dare do anything. You can count on me to help,' Lindy said. 'You're my best friend. I won't let you down. I've already got an idea. Why don't you put on your mask and see what he wants?'

8

Anna knocked on the storeroom door.

'Wait!' the new lord shouted.

She waited. Shifted from one foot to the other and yawned. Minutes passed. What was he doing in there? Trying to make her nervous? If so, he was succeeding.

I don't like him, she thought. I don't like the way his eyes glitter. I don't like his sneering voice, and the smell of him, stale and smoky and odd –

There were noises behind the locked door. A thud. Voices. Something scraped and banged across the floor. Someone laughed.

'The others are very late,' Lindy said, coming in from the front. 'I've been looking up and down the road and there's no sign of them.'

'They're in there,' Anna said. 'I can hear them. They came in the back way.'

Lindy darted across to the storeroom door and listened.

'Jeremy must've got some keys cut – and never gave me one. Beast!'

She knocked loudly on the door and darted away again, leaving Anna, taken by surprise, standing there stupidly when it opened, and the lords of the Som came out.

They were all cloaked and hooded in their different colours, and their eyes stared at her through the holes in their masks. She wished she too had a full mask to hide behind, instead of the narrow one that was all a mere companion was allowed. It made her feel conspicuous to be the only one with half her face showing.

'Stand back,' the fat Red Lord said in his high pitched voice. 'Make way for the Goldmaster of the Som.'

She stepped back meekly, but it was no good. They stopped in front of her.

'My first companion,' the Yellow Lord said, laughing and pointing at her with a gloved finger. 'What have I done to deserve her, Goldmaster? Still, I suppose it's a challenge.' He turned back to Anna and looked her up and down. 'Your hair's a mess,' he said, 'and as for your clothes – you look ridiculous. I've seen stupid things printed on tee shirts before, but really – "Dracula rules OK",' he read out. 'Tell me, is that part of the campaign to save the bat from extinction?'

Everybody laughed. Even Lindy, her friend, tittered behind her silver mask.

'I like it,' Anna said, refusing to be intimidated. 'It was a present from the Vampires at my last school. I wasn't a member but I made up a code for them and they gave me one of their shirts in return. And promised never to drink my blood,' she added, smiling.

Everyone laughed again, but this time they were laughing with her. She looked at the Yellow Lord to see how he liked that.

He didn't. His paper face remained blank but he had no mask to hide the anger in his voice. 'What an exciting life you've led,' he drawled. 'You must find us very tame by comparison. Never mind. We'll have to see what we can do about that. I know. I'll set you your first task. The skylight in the passage outside is filthy. You're to clean it before the swearing-in on Saturday. Properly. Both sides of the glass, inside and out.'

'But how can I reach it? It's so high up – and I don't think it opens.'

'That'll make it a more interesting problem, won't it? I hope it doesn't prove to be beyond your mental capacity, Birdie, because if you fail, you'll be punished. It's in the rules.'

'What rules?' Anna asked, but he had walked away, taking the other lords with him. Only the Red Lord stayed with her to say gleefully:

'The new rules. We're always making them up. That's what we do in our secret councils, think up horrible things for the companions to do. Tasks and tests and punishments. It's great fun.'

'It sounds it.'

'Well, we got to do something. To tell the truth, it's a bit boring sometimes. I mean, it's so dark and stuffy in here.' He looked round the shadowy, candle-lit room with dissatisfaction. 'No telly. No table tennis or nothing like that. There's cards, of course, but they've started playing for money and we're not all millionaires. I don't see no fun in losing all my pocket money in one go. You're lucky they won't allow companions to play.'

'You don't have to. Lindy doesn't.'

'Her! She did once, and cried when she lost. I don't want them thinking I'm soft. What are you grinning at? You watch yourself, Birdie, or I'll pluck all your feathers out.'

She laughed. She wasn't frightened of him. She knew who he was. Duncan Stretton, who sang in the choir on Sundays, dressed up in a white surplice like an angel. It was no good his pretending to be a red devil now. What would the vicar think?

She was tempted to say, 'See you on Sunday,' but he had walked off. She looked round. Lindy was in the group round the table, complaining about something. 'I don't think it's fair,' she was saying. 'I was here before you.'

'I should never have let her join,' the Goldmaster said. Anna jumped and looked round. He was standing just behind her. 'Nor you either. You're both too young.'

Her heart beat faster and she couldn't speak. He looked so strange and beautiful in his golden mask. It was impossible to remember he was only Lindy's brother.

'Do you understand about the tasks, Birdie?' he asked.

'Not – not exactly.'

'Think of them as a challenge. I want the Som to grow. To become something big. To do any good, you have to have power or people can push you about. You have to be strong. That's what the tasks are for, to train you companions to be brave and obedient and quick-witted. Do you understand?'

'Um – I think so.'

'Every companion is to be set ten tasks, each more difficult than the last. If he performs them satisfactorily, he becomes a lord of the Som. Or in your case, a lady. Wouldn't you like to be the Yellow Lady of the Som, Birdie?'

'I'd rather be a lady of any other colour,' she muttered.

He looked at her, and asked softly, 'Which colour would you like best?'

She was about to say silver, for all the boys teased her and though Lindy was bossy, at least she was used to her. But something made her hesitate. She sensed he expected a different answer.

'Gold,' she said.

'So you want to be gold. That's ambitious of you,' he said, but she could tell he was pleased, for he laughed indulgently. 'I hope you're not planning to oust me from my position.'

'No. I just wanted to – to – '

'To serve me? To be my true and loyal companion?'

'Yes.'

He laughed again and ruffled her hair with his hand. 'I'm afraid that's impossible, Birdie. I'm the Goldmaster. I have the lords as my companions, and you must serve a lord. You've no complaints against the Lord of the Yellow, have you?'

The new lord was his friend.

'No,' she said.

'Why did you hesitate? You can confide in me. I shall always listen.'

'It's nothing,' she said, raising her voice for she'd seen the Lord of the Yellow watching them. 'Thank you, Goldmaster, but there's nothing.'

'Good,' he said, and walked away.

After all, what could I have said? she wondered. That I hate Lord Mustard-face? That he gives me the shivers? He'd only have laughed at me. . . .

'It's perfect,' Lindy said, as they were walking home together. 'It couldn't be better. It fits my plan like it was made for it.'

'What does?'

'The task he set you.'

'Task?'

'What's the matter with you? You seem half asleep. The task. You know, cleaning the skylight. Can't you see? It'll give you the perfect excuse to get up on to the roof.'

'I don't want to get up on to the roof,' Anna said. 'How can I? I'd need a ladder.'

'Oh, ladders. Ladders are easy. Plenty of ladders about. We've got three at home. Aluminium. Easy to carry. We can manage even the longest between us without trouble. The hard part will be getting it out of the house without anyone noticing. But once we get to the factory, we'll be all set. The perfect excuse. Anybody says anything, you can tell them you're just cleaning the skylight.'

'I will be just cleaning the skylight, won't I?' Anna asked, puzzled.

61

'Honestly, Anna. You're so thick. You always have to have everything spelt out to you. The skylight's not important. It's being up on the roof when the Yellow Lord arrives for the swearing-in. He'll come in the back way, thinking himself safe. He won't guess you're up on the roof hiding behind that sort of ventilator thing. You'll be able to see his face. What I thought was, you could take a camera – '

'Lindy, I can't – '

'Of course you can. It's a flat roof. You'll be perfectly comfortable. And when he's gone, I'll let you down so you won't miss the swearing-in. Anna, you can't refuse to do a little thing like that for me?'

9

On Friday Anna was to spend the night with Lindy. Her grandmother had bought her a new nightdress; white with pink roses and ribbons, and puff sleeves edged with lace. The sort of thing Anna had longed for when she was younger. Much younger. Lindy would sneer at it.

'We can't have you sleeping in one of those terrible old shirts you insist upon wearing in bed,' Mrs Cotman said. 'What would Mrs Miller think?'

'King,' Anna said. 'She's Mrs King now. She married again.'

'Oh yes, you did tell me. And I've seen them together in church. Poor man, I don't think he has an easy time of it.'

'Why?'

'Oh – just something about the way they all treat him. Like he was a dog with fleas.'

'I know, but . . . he's a property developer. Lindy says nobody likes him.'

'What nonsense,' her grandmother said sharply. 'There's good and bad property developers, I suppose, like in any other job. A lot of people like him. The vicar does for one,' she added with a smile. 'They say

Harry King gave him a hundred pounds for the restoration fund.'

'Cupboard love!' Anna exclaimed, with a sneer Lindy would have been proud of. 'That's what that is. Lindy says – '

'Lindy, Lindy! I'm sick of hearing you parrot Lindy. Judge people for yourself, Anna. Don't let her tell you what to think. You've got a mind of your own, I hope. You don't need her.'

'She needs me,' Anna said. 'Nobody else will put up with her – I'm only joking, Gran,' she added hastily, seeing her grandmother's expression.

'Sounded very like the truth to me,' Mrs Cotman said drily. Then she smiled and hugged Anna. 'Have a lovely weekend. I shall miss you. What are you planning to do?'

'Oh, this and that,' Anna said vaguely.

She could hardly tell Gran that tomorrow, early in the morning before the birds were awake, she and Lindy were going to creep out of Harry King's house, and carry his best expanding ladder through the empty streets of the town.

'You'll have to climb up to the roof before anybody's about,' Lindy had said. 'You know how interfering people are. They'll want to know what you're doing, and when you tell them, they'll say you can't. People are so fussy. They'd be afraid you'd fall off.'

Anna was afraid she'd fall off, too, but Lindy told her not to be so silly. The roof, she claimed, was only four metres from the ground. Or five.

'Even if you did fall off,' she said reassuringly, 'you

wouldn't break anything really serious. Only a leg or two.'

In the morning, a thin grey drizzle filled the air and made the pavements shine.

'It's raining,' Anna said.

They were standing outside the Hall of Secrets. It was twenty past six and all sensible people were still in bed.

'You can't call this rain,' Lindy told her. 'It's mist. River mist.'

'It's wet.'

'No. Not very. Hardly at all. What a fuss you're making, Anna. Anyone would think you're an old woman. I suppose it comes from being brought up by your grandmother. Rainwater's supposed to be good for your complexion.'

'I'll drown up there. I'll die of pneumonia.'

'No, you won't,' Lindy said firmly. 'You've got your anorak on – you can put up the hood and be quite cosy. I put lots of food in your bag; sandwiches, apples, cake. . . . And a couple of books and a pack of cards. You'll have a lovely time. Look, it's beginning to clear up already. You can almost see the sun.'

And indeed, in the east, the misty sky was brightening into a pale gold. Perhaps it wouldn't be too bad. At least she'd be able to finish cleaning the skylight, and that would be her first task done. Only nine more to do and she'd be the Lady of the Yellow, able to give herself airs and boss the poor companions around.

'Hold the ladder steady,' she said, and climbed up.

The roof, she found, was not absolutely flat. There was a low parapet at the front, from which it sloped gently to the gutter at the back. It had a rough surface, patched with moss and speckled with gravel and bits of rubble. On the right side, a few feet from the gutter, there was a ventilation hood, about the size of a dog's kennel. It was behind this that she was to hide and take photographs of the Yellow Lord when he arrived, unmasked and unsuspecting. A small pool of water had collected in front of it, just where she was supposed to lie down.

'I can see you!' Lindy called.

Anna looked down. 'I can see you, too.'

'You'll have to sit down or people will spot you from the street.'

'The roof's wet.'

'Don't fuss.'

Anna walked a few steps away from the edge and crouched down.

'That better?'

'A bit further — that's fine. I can't see you now. Stay like that.'

For ten hours? Anna thought sourly.

From where she sat, she could only see the outer half of the yard at the back. The high wall hid the road beyond, but the upper windows of the houses opposite were visible. The curtains were drawn. Soon the alarm clocks would wake the sleepers. Already there were noises in the street behind her. A car went by. Something banged and scraped. People would go to their windows and draw back the curtains to see what sort of a day it was. They would see her. Lindy hadn't thought of that.

She turned and crawled back to the parapet. When she looked down into the street, the pavement was empty. No Lindy –

No ladder!

'Lindy!' she shrieked.

Lindy came out of the workshop and looked up innocently.

'What have you done with the ladder?' Anna asked.

'I took it down, of course. What did you think I was going to do with it – leave it there for people to trip over? I've put it in the passage. Don't worry. As soon as the Yellow Lord comes in, I'll bring it out again. I'll get you down in time for the swearing-in, I promise. I'd better go now.'

'Don't forget me!' Anna called, as her friend began walking away down the street.

'You can count on me!' Lindy cried, looking back and waving.

The sun, breaking through the mist, made a thin silhouette of her, sharp and black against the shining pavement.

By one o'clock, the last of the mist had cleared away, and it was hot. The sun had dried up the puddles on the roof and the moss was warm. Anna lay on her back and looked up at the blue sky. She was bored.

She had already eaten all the sandwiches, read one of the books and played two games of patience, neither of which came out. The slight slope of the roof made it difficult to get comfortable. And because

67

she knew she mustn't stand up, it was the one thing she longed to do. Her legs ached to be vertical.

She sat up and began to eat an apple. The curtains were drawn back now in the windows of the houses opposite, but nobody had looked out to point and exclaim. Perhaps she looked like an ink-blot in her blue shirt and trousers. Perhaps they didn't care how many girls sat on the roof all day.

She crawled towards the parapet and looked over. There was nobody in sight. The old woman who owned the junk shop had put some furniture out on the pavement; chairs with cane seats, a long narrow table on which there was a tray of oddments, a straw hat with a pink ostrich feather and an enormous brass pot. Anna aimed her apple-core at the pot and missed. It hit instead a blue jug, knocking it on to the pavement. The jug broke. A small black cat, startled, shot out from under the table, streaked across the street and under the feet of a child who came running round the corner. The child sat down heavily and began to howl.

Anna ducked down and wriggled back towards the ventilation hood.

It just shows how careful you have to be, she thought. You do one simple thing and you never know where it will end. Like me and my apple-core. Like Harry King, trying to please his cold, pretty wife by being kind to her son. He gives him a key – and that's how it all began. One thing after another, the box of masks, the Som, the terrible oath. . . . And who's going to be the child who ends up howling? Me?

She lay back on the roof and closed her eyes. Time passed. The sun crawled across the arc of the sky like a bright snail. Anna slept.

The Lord of the Yellow came at ten past five. Anna was ready for him, lying behind the ventilation hood, camera in hand. She heard the noise of the motorcycle in the road behind the high wall. Heard it stop. She looked round the edge of the hood and saw the gate open and a figure appear. It wore a black denim jacket and a black and yellow crash helmet, with the visor down. There was another figure behind it in the gateway, carrying a cardboard carton. This one too was wearing a crash helmet, white and red. The lower half of his face was bearded.

'OK?' the bearded man said, and handed over the carton.

'Fine.'

'See you later.'

'Right.'

The bearded man went away. The other shut and locked the door after him. Then he turned. The lower half of his face was covered by a yellow silk scarf and he was wearing pale yellow gloves. He shut and locked the gate after him, then turned and came towards her.

He had beaten them, the Lord of the Yellow.

No point in taking a photo. At least, better take one to show Lindy she hadn't just fallen asleep. She pressed the button.

The slight click was scarcely audible, but immediately he looked up, as if stung by a wasp.

Anna ducked back behind the ventilator hood as soon as she saw his head begin to turn up, but she didn't know if she'd been in time. She crouched, hugging her arms, trying to make herself as small as possible. She could not hear him. No sound of footsteps. No door opening. She waited. Then she heard him laugh, and walk away.

10

At half past six that evening, the last grinning, blindfolded boy was led by one of the lords down the pavement and into the workshop. Nine boys were already in the passage, lined up against the wall, waiting for the swearing-in to begin. Some of them still grinned uneasily. One giggled, and was told off sharply by the Blue Lord.

'Silence! The oath of the Som is no laughing matter.'

'What is it, then?' someone muttered, and the Blue Lord demanded angrily, 'Who said that? Who was it?'

They shuffled and did not answer.

'It'll soon be too late to draw back,' the Blue Lord warned them. 'You'd better speak up now if you're afraid to go on with it. Well? Have we any cowards here?'

Nobody spoke.

Anna tapped on the glass of the skylight.

The Blue Lord looked up. He didn't seem surprised to see a figure silhouetted against the bright sky, but merely made an impatient gesture with his hand, as if brushing her away. Stubbornly Anna knocked again.

'Let me in,' she said.

He waved her away once more, and when she did not move, went over and opened the workroom door. Below her, the line of waiting boys shuffled and whispered, then fell silent.

The Lord of the Yellow came out into the passage and looked up. He was masked and hooded, his long robe bright as a daffodil in the patch of sunlight. Though the boys could not see him and he did not speak, the chill of his presence seemed to fall on them, for they became as quiet as stone. He stood, staring up at Anna.

She looked back at him defiantly, her heart thumping.

'Let me in, my lord,' she said. 'I've done the task you set me. The skylight's clean.'

At first she thought he wasn't going to answer, and she leaned forward over the glass. Her shadow fell on him, and he stepped back quickly.

'No,' he said coldly. 'You will stay up there in silence until it pleases the lords to let you down. This is the second task I set you. If you break your silence or draw attention to yourself in any way, you will have failed.'

With that, he turned and went back into the workroom.

The boys whispered and tilted their faces upwards as if hoping to see her through their blindfolds. The Blue Lord waved his hand dismissively, and Anna drew back out of sight.

She sat down by the ventilation hood and rested her chin on her hands. It wasn't Lindy's fault, after all. She hadn't just forgotten her. The Yellow Lord had probably confiscated the ladder and forbidden anyone to let her down. No wonder the Blue Lord hadn't been surprised to see her there. He'd been told. They'd all been told.

How long did they mean to keep her up there? All night?

Why not? One summer's night and she'd have done her second task. Was it so terrible? Gran wasn't expecting her back. Lindy could tell Mrs King some tale. Nobody would miss her.

Supposing she rolled off the roof in her sleep?

She sighed. It was her choice. If she stood up and shouted loudly enough, somebody would hear her. There were houses opposite. Somebody must live in them, and would come –

The Goldmaster would be disappointed in her. He admired loyalty and courage. The words of her favourite hymn came into her mind –

'Who would true valour see,
Let him come hither,
Here's one who'll constant be,
Come wind, come weather . . .'

I'll do it, she thought. I'll stay here, even if it pours with rain. Even if there's a thunderstorm. She shivered, and sat with her arms wrapped around her, while the sun sank lower in the sky and a small wind came up, cool with the threat of night.

Someone began to scream.

The sound came from below, piercing and so oddly regular that at first she almost thought it was a whistle. But then the rhythm broke up into shrill, yelping sobs, and she heard the word 'No!' ring out in terror.

She got up and ran to the parapet. The street below was empty.

'Lindy!' she shouted.

The sobs cut off abruptly. Silence. No windows opened in the houses opposite. They either hadn't heard, or didn't care.

'Lindy! Lindy!'

Why didn't someone come? Were they all dead down there? Was she the only person left in the world?

'LINDY!'

Below her, the door opened and Lindy came out. She looked up and down the street, and then up at Anna. 'Wait a minute,' she said. 'Can't you see I'm busy.'

She went back into the building, only to appear again almost immediately, carrying one end of the ladder. The Red Lord was carrying the other.

'It wasn't my fault,' he was saying. 'How was I to know he'd have hysterics. They can't blame me. You all agreed to it.'

'Oh, shut up!' Lindy snapped.

'What's happened?' Anna demanded, but they were lifting up the ladder and didn't answer. When they spoke, it was only to tell her to come down now and be quick about it, before anyone came.

'It was the entrails what done it,' the Red Lord said. 'And them soft eggs – you know, ain't you ever cleaned a chicken? All that stinking straw and blood and stuff, that's what set him off. Gawd knows what he thought they were.'

'There'll be trouble about this,' Lindy said.

'No, there won't. They'll fix it so he won't dare open his little mouth.'

'Who? Who screamed? What have you done to him?' Anna cried, stepping off the ladder on to the pavement.

'Nothing. Just a bit of fun. You girls had better be off. Leave it to us.'

'Leave what? Is someone hurt? *What have you done?*'

'Gawd,' the Red Lord muttered. 'Take her away, Lindy. We got enough on our plate without her squawking. What d'you think we're doing to him, Birdie? We're trying to calm him down, aren't we? There's the Goldmaster holding his sticky little hand and stroking his greasy hair. Be a good girl and go off with Lindy.'

'I won't! I want to see for myself that he's all right. I won't go – '

'Yes, you will,' Lindy said, grasping her arm so tightly that it hurt. 'Take the ladder back inside before you're seen,' she said to the Red Lord. 'We'll fetch it later. You can leave Anna to me.'

'No, he can't!' Anna shouted, struggling furiously to free herself. But Lindy was too strong for her. She held Anna until the Red Lord had disappeared with the ladder, and shut the door behind him. Anna heard the key turn in the lock.

'There,' Lindy said, letting her go. 'Now you can't get in, so you might as well stop making an ass of yourself. Who d'you think you are? Florence Nightingale? The little drip wasn't hurt, anyway, just scared out of his tiny mind. Nobody laid a finger on him. It was that stupid bucket of butcher's muck — the moment he put his hand in, he started yelling and trying to tear off his blindfold. And the trouble was, he hadn't taken his oath yet. Still, the lords will fix him.'

'What do you mean?' Anna asked, staring at the locked door in horror. 'What are they planning to do?'

'Nothing. Keep your hair on. Jeremy's nursing the baby, all soft soap and what a brave boy you are. Jeremy's good at that. He'll have the little twerp eating out of his hand in no time. Then when he's taken his oath, they've got him for life. He won't dare break it any more than we would. Would we?' she asked, giggling uneasily. 'We wouldn't, would we, Anna?'

Anna didn't answer. She stared at the Hall of Secrets. Nobody screamed. Nobody cried out for help. It was quiet now. The Goldmaster was good at nursing babies. The little twerp — was that how he thought of her, too? Soft soap for Anna. Soft soap for the screaming boy. . . .

'Come on, Anna,' Lindy said coaxingly. 'He's all right, honestly. You can trust me.'

'Can I?'

'Don't be like that. It wasn't my fault you missed it all. You let the Yellow Lord see you — I warned you not to! He said if we let you down, something horrid would happen to us. I wouldn't have left you there all night, honest, even if he hadn't changed his mind and told us to get you away. So you needn't sulk. Come on, I'll treat you to fish and chips on the way home. And you can have a chocolate whirlpool.'

'I don't want one,' Anna said.

She turned and walked with Lindy down the street. But when Lindy tried to take her arm, she pulled it away.

11

'That's him! Look, over there, just coming out of Woolworth's.'

Anna looked where Lindy was pointing and saw a skinny boy, with lank, flaxen hair and one of those fair skins that go bright pink in the sun and then peel. Peter Elkin's skin was peeling now. There were whitish flakes on his cheeks and forehead, but no bruises, no blood.

'Not a mark on him,' Lindy said. 'I told you they wouldn't hurt him, didn't I? Now perhaps you'll stop going around with that funeral face. Anyone would think we'd murdered him, the way you carried on.'

The boy was hesitating on the pavement, looking up and down the street with quick turns of the head. His eyes were grey and looked glassy. There were dark smudges under them.

'He looks frightened,' Anna said.

'There you go again! If you ask me, he scares easy. He probably never got over the shock of being born. Or perhaps he's nicked something from Woolworth's and is afraid of getting caught. Stop worrying about him, Anna. It's nothing to do with us.'

'I suppose not,' Anna said.

She looked after him as he walked away. His head drooped forward on his thin neck. He looked very young and sad and defenceless.

'I suppose it's nothing to do with us,' she repeated.

Yet in the months that followed, she watched out for him. She did not see him often at school, for he was a first-former and she had moved up into 2A. He was seldom in the playground and always hurried away when school was over, walking by himself with his shoulders hunched, as if expecting at any moment to be stabbed in the back.

Once, glancing through a window at lunchtime, she saw him sitting at his desk in the empty classroom, his head resting on his hands. She slipped away from Lindy and went to find him. He looked up nervously when she opened the door, mumbled something and looked back at the book on his desk.

'Hullo,' she said.

He looked up again and said almost inaudibly: 'Hullo.'

'What are you reading?'

He pushed the book over to her. She saw a photograph of two polar bears posed against a landscape of ice. 'I got it from the library,' he said in nervous haste, as if defending himself against an unspoken accusation. The left side of his face kept twitching.

'Are you all right?' she asked, for he looked ill.

'Yes. Yes, I am.'

She perched on the edge of the desk next to his, and wondered what to do next.

'I am all right,' he insisted. 'I never said I wasn't. I never complained. Don't tell them I did.'

He was frightened of her. He had seen her in the Hall of Secrets and had recognised her here.

'You know me, don't you?' she said. 'What gave me away? My voice? My freckles?'

Unlike the lords, the companions wore narrow masks, covering only the upper half of their faces, so that many of them were recognisable. They wore their ordinary clothes too, the only rule being that they must wear a scarf or a band round their wrists to show the colour of the lord they followed.

When at the Som, Anna wore a silver mask and a silver bracelet, for her allegiance had been changed. She was the Silver Bird now, and served the Silver Lady. Lindy claimed this was all her doing, but Anna didn't believe her. It was the Goldmaster who had told her of the change, and asked her kindly if she was pleased. He had been sorry for her, as she in her turn was sorry for the boys who had to wear the yellow.

Like little Peter Elkin, with his twitching face and frightened eyes.

'Don't be scared of me,' she said now. 'I'm on your side. I was a companion of the yellow once, and I hated it. Does he bully you? Would you like me to ask the Goldmaster if you can change your colour?'

'No! I like it!' he cried, looking more terrified than ever. 'I do! I haven't complained. You can't say I've complained!' With that he burst into tears.

Dismayed, Anna put her arm round his shoulders and promised she wouldn't tell anyone anything, not if he didn't want her to.

'Only do stop crying. The bell will be going soon and you don't want people to see you all blotchy. You can trust me, honestly. Look, have my hanky.'

The boy took it, with mumbled thanks, and wiped his face and eyes obediently.

'That's it,' she said. 'I'd better go now.' When she reached the door, she turned back and added: 'Remember, I'm your friend. If ever you're in trouble, come and tell me. I'll stick up for you.'

He looked at her with amazement, then gave her a small, doubtful smile.

That was the beginning of an odd, secretive friendship between them – if friendship wasn't too big a word for what was usually only an exchange of smiles when no one was watching. Once or twice, when they met on the common or by the river and there was no one they knew in sight, they would talk a little.

'How's things, Peter?'

'All right.'

'Caught any fish?'

'No. Got one last week, though.'

'Good for you.'

Anna was pleased, feeling she was winning the trust of some shy, wild creature.

In the Hall of Secrets, they each, without consulting each other, behaved like strangers. Peter in his yellow mask, walked with his head bowed and his eyes fixed on the ground, only looking up if the Lord of the

Yellow called him, when he would hurry trembling, to see what was wanted. Anna, knowing this lord disliked her all the more since she'd slipped out of his reach, was careful to show no interest in Peter. She never jumped to his defence when he was being teased, in case she made things worse for him. Instead she would do something foolish – knock over a candle-jar and shriek as the candle rolled over the floor, or spill the red wine over one of the lords.

'You've become terribly clumsy, Anna,' Lindy complained. 'You never used to be like this. You can't blame the lords for shouting at you. I mean, I do my best for you, but really, you must be more careful.'

'I'm sorry,' Anna said meekly.

'And you ought to call me "my lady" in here. After all, you are my companion. I wouldn't bother if it was just for myself – I don't mind what you call me, but the lords were saying only the other day that you ought to call me "my lady".'

'Yes, my lady.'

Lindy looked at her. Her silver mask hid her face, but her voice sounded suspicious when she said: 'You're not going to sulk, are you?'

'No, my lady. Of course not, my lady. I wouldn't dream of it, my lady.'

'Pig,' Lindy said crossly.

Anna smiled. Turning away, she caught sight of Peter standing in a shadowy corner. He was looking straight at her and their eyes met. Then they both turned away.

Two weeks later they broke up for Christmas. Anna walked with Lindy as far as her house, but refused to come in as she'd promised her grandmother she'd be back early. As she walked on towards the wool shop, a small figure suddenly stepped out of a doorway and thrust something into her hands.

'Peter! Don't go!' she cried, for he was already turning away.

'It's nothing much,' he said awkwardly, meaning the small, gold-wrapped parcel in her hands. 'Don't think you've got to give me something back. It's not just for Christmas, it's a sort of, well – thank you present.'

'Thank you for what?' she asked, puzzled.

'Did you think I hadn't noticed? Whenever they were getting at me, you did something to make them shout at you instead. I dunno why you did it, Anna. You're a girl. It ought to be me protecting you.'

'I'm older than you,' she said, laughing and embarrassed. 'Think of me as your older sister.'

He muttered something she didn't hear, something about a friend, and fled away down the street.

Inside the gold-wrapped parcel was a small red box, and in the box was a tiny silver heart on a silver chain as fine as a cobweb.

12

After Christmas, the weather turned very cold. The paraffin heater scarcely warmed the Hall of Secrets. They sat round it in their coats and scarves and gloves, and shivered. Peter's small face grew thinner and paler than ever. Anna worried in case he became ill.

'You ought to ask Harry to get the electricity reconnected,' she told Lindy. 'He can't have meant you to freeze in here. I expect he forgot – '

'Of course he forgot,' Lindy said. 'He only gave Jeremy the key to show Mum what a good stepfather he is. Him! He makes me sick. A proper father would've kept an eye on us. Not Harry. He can't forget us quickly enough.'

Anna was silent. Judge for yourself, Gran had said, so she watched Harry King carefully whenever she saw him. He had a nice smile. He told her his favourite subject at school had been history. He ate quickly and neatly. He didn't like carrots. What sort of person did that add up to? Carrots were supposed to help you see in the dark, or so Gran said. Perhaps he didn't want to see his new family too clearly. Perhaps that was why he'd never been round to the

Hall of Secrets. . . .Lindy said he was horrid and she ought to know, and yet he had seemed kind.

'You could remind him,' she suggested.

Lindy shrieked at that. 'Anna, you're so silly! I meant he *ought* to've remembered, I didn't mean we wanted him to. The very last thing we want is Harry coming round to see what we're getting up to.'

'What are we getting up to?' Anna asked slowly.

'Ah, that'd be telling,' Lindy said and giggled, but Anna thought she did not know either.

Something was going on behind their backs. People stopped talking when they came into the room. People came to the Hall of Secrets on the days when she and Lindy had been told there was no meeting. There were signs left lying about that Lindy, being the Silver Lady, was too grand to see. It was Anna who swept the floor, and noticed chalk marks that had not been there before. Anna who found fresh scratches on top of the long work-tables. Anna who saw the five large hooks that appeared in the ceiling.

'What are those for?' she had asked Lindy.

'How should I know? Must've been there when we came.'

'No. They're new. They weren't there last week.'

'They must've been. Honestly, Anna, you are daft. Why should we put them there? I suppose you think we're going to start hanging the companions who fail their tasks. Like little lemon-face over there – '

She meant Peter Elkin. He *was* terribly pale. His skin, which looked yellowish in the candle-light, looked almost blue-white in the street outside.

'You ought to wrap up more,' Anna told him,

85

when they met by chance near the wool shop. 'Haven't you got a warmer coat?'

He flushed painfully and shook his head. Perhaps his family are poor, she thought, and went on quickly, 'I expect you're growing out of your clothes like I am, and it's not really worth getting a new coat when it's nearly spring, is it?'

'Spring?' he repeated and smiled, looking round at the icy streets and the hedges white with frost.

'I've got an old duffle coat I've grown out of. You could have that if you like,' she said, not looking at him in case he blushed again.

'Yes. Yes, please,' he said eagerly, as if he believed there would be some magic in it, some courage left in the pockets, some charm to protect him whenever he wore it.

'I'm afraid it isn't new,' she said, 'but it's warm, and it'll be big on you, so you can wear lots of things underneath. It's so cold there, isn't it?'

'He doesn't let us stay cold for long,' Peter said. 'He keeps us at it – you know, the toughening-up. He says you've got to go on until it hurts and you drown in your own sweat. He wants us to win. He says we've got to win.'

'Win what? What are you talking about?'

'The games. The summer games.' Seeing her look puzzled, he asked anxiously, 'Didn't you know about the games? Don't tell them I told you! Please, Anna!'

'Of course I won't.'

'I'm sorry. It's just . . . I always think they'll hear us talking,' he said, glancing over his shoulder at the empty street. 'I always expect to see them behind me.'

She took him to a small café. They sat in the corner on red plastic seats, warming their hands round cups of hot chocolate, feeling safe. The windows were misted up and the only other customer was an old lady nodding over her tea. The girl behind the counter was reading a thriller and paid no attention to them.

'Tell me about the games,' Anna said.

'The Yellow Lord told us. He says there's to be challenges and – and personal combat. The others say I'll be no good at it. They say I'll let the Yellows down.' He looked at her with sad, anxious eyes. 'And the Yellow Lord says if I do, he'll punish me. He's cross with me already. I failed my first task.'

'What was it?' Anna asked, but he refused to tell her.

'I can't,' he said, looking frightened. 'It's not allowed. You're not a Yellow. I can't tell you. Don't ask me, Anna, please don't.'

'All right,' she said, shrugging.

They were silent for a moment. Peter kept glancing at her.

'You're not cross, are you?' he said at last.

'No.'

'I would tell you, only I'm frightened. If he found out, he'd punish me. Do you know what he did when I failed my task? It was Thursday, remember how cold it was, with ice on all the puddles? He made me go into the yard and stand in a bowl of freezing water. It really was freezing. I had to break the ice. He kept me there for ages. I couldn't feel my feet any more, and I heard my teeth chattering. The others laughed. Then he told me to run round the yard till my feet were warm again, but I couldn't. My feet were numb and I fell over.'

'He's mad!' Anna said. 'You might've got pneumonia. You might've died. Somebody should stop him. I'll tell the Goldmaster – '

'No! You mustn't! I don't want you to,' he cried out, so loudly that the old lady and the girl behind the counter stared at him. 'Please, Anna,' he said, lowering his voice, 'I don't really mind. It's good for me. It's part of the toughening-up. It didn't do me any harm. My feet didn't fall off – look, there they are,' he said, smiling, trying to make a joke of it. 'And it'll make me strong. That's what they all say. If we get through it, it'll make us strong. Don't you think I look better already?'

'No, you look like a ghost. You ought to leave the Som.'

'I can't,' he whispered. 'It's too late. I've taken the oath. You can't get away when you've taken the oath, can you? Not ever.'

'You cried out in your sleep last night, Anna,' Mrs Cotman said.

'I had a bad dream.'

'Another one? That's the second this week. Are you worried about anything, love? You're not in trouble at school, are you?'

'No.'

She wished she could tell Gran. She wanted to talk things over with someone sensible, almost anyone would do – she even thought of Harry King. But it was no good. She was helpless as a fly in a spider's web, caught fast in the threads of too many oaths and promises she could not break. She could tell no one.

Something was wrong, but she didn't know what. Whenever she saw Peter and asked him how he was, he said all right, but his eyes were still frightened. He would not tell her any more.

After her third nightmare, Anna went round to the Red Lord's house and knocked on the door as bold, he told her crossly, as flipping brass.

'You're not supposed to know who I am. And what's my mum going to think, girls calling at our house this early? It's bad for my reputation. Go away.'

'I've got to ask someone.'

'Why pick on me?'

'You sing in the choir at church. There must be some good in you somewhere.'

He smiled at that, but told her he sang for money.

'We get paid for weddings and special occasions, see? Still as you're here, you'd better come in. But only for a minute, mind.'

He took her into a small dining-room. The table was covered with clean washing, some already ironed, in neat piles, the rest piled high in a red plastic basket, and overflowing. The chairs had been pushed to one side to make room for an ironing board. He licked his finger and touched the upended iron.

'Stone cold,' he said. 'Poor Mum. Dad gave her a new washing machine for her birthday. Thirty programmes. She washed everything in sight. She'd have washed me if I hadn't dodged. Now she's so sick of the ironing, she hasn't been in here for days and we have to eat off trays. We'll be quite private in here. You said you wanted to ask me something about the Som. Go ahead. Ask.'

'What are those hooks for?' she blurted out.

He stared at her, then a huge smile spread over his face.

'You mean the meat hooks? They're for hanging things. Like you, Birdie. We're going to hang you up by your feet, like a silly goose for Easter.'

'Very funny.'

'I think it is,' he said, and as if to prove it, laughed so long and loud that tears ran down his fat cheeks.

She waited patiently till he had finished, and then asked again:

'Come on, Red. Tell me.'

'They're for a climbing net,' he told her, wiping his eyes on a clean but crumpled hanky from the table. 'I bet you thought it was for torture. I bet you did.'

'I wouldn't have been surprised. What else do they do for the toughening-up?'

He shrugged. 'Whatever their lords tell 'em to do.'

'What do you tell them?'

'Just the usual. Press-ups and sit-ups and running on the spot.'

'Is that what the Yellows do?' she asked, but he told her he had no idea.

'We all come at different times,' he explained. 'Each lord has his own band of companions to train. We don't see the others except at the general meetings. Why didn't you ask the Silver Lady? Isn't she putting you in for the games?' He grinned, and added, 'I'd like to see that.'

'You won't. She's cross because nobody told her about the games. And she won't set me any more tasks. She keeps saying she hasn't time to think of any. I've only done two.'

'Doesn't want you to become another Silver Lady. Can't say I blame her. One's enough. Come to that, I don't want my lot becoming lords. There'd be no one left for me to boss about. There're too many lords as it is. There were two new ones at the inner council meeting last week. Found them sitting there, as cool as cucumbers. Dunno who they were. Nobody's told me. Everything's so secret now, it gets confusing. I sat next to the one in the purple mask. "Hullo, Purp, where've you sprung from," I ask, just to be friendly. Know what he said, the snotty swab? "Please don't call me by that nauseating abbreviation. I am the Lord of the Purple." "And I'm the Lord of the Red," I tell him, "and I'll give you a red nose any time you like."'

'That was telling him,' Anna said.

The Red Lord gave a sheepish grin. 'Yeah, only I waited till he'd moved out of earshot before I come out with it. You haven't seen him, Birdie. He's big. Twice my size.'

'Who invited them to join?'

'Dunno. Not me. I was going to ask the Goldmaster, but they hung round him like he was a honeypot. Talk about smarm and charm, they were ladling it over him. And of course he was lapping it up – '

'The Goldmaster? Why? What did he say?'

She shouldn't have said anything. It reminded him

he was talking to a mere companion, and a girl, at that.

'Never you mind,' he told her. 'You forget what I said or you'll get me into trouble. We're not supposed to tell the companions more than they need to know. And all you need to know now is – I want you out of here. Fly away, Birdie. I got better things to do than talk to you.'

'But –'

'Don't argue. You shouldn't have come here. Run along and try to keep your nose clean. The Yellow Lord's got it in for you, and he's not a person I'd care to tangle with. Don't give him a chance to catch you breaking the rules.'

'I won't,' Anna said.

He smiled. 'You're not a bad kid, Birdie. Take care of yourself.'

'I will.'

She was careful at first. She walked warily, avoiding the cracks in the pavement, crossing her fingers when she saw the Yellow Lord and touching wood. But when the weeks passed and nothing terrible happened, she began to forget her fears. She became careless.

13

It was a hot day in July when it happened. A day for swimming in the river, not for sitting in a drowsy classroom. Anna chewed the end of her biro. What was the French for library? Bible ... biblo ... biblio-something. She frowned, made a wild guess and wrote down firmly, *bibliomaison*. It looked wrong. Out of the corner of her eye, she saw that Lindy was peeking again. All she'd get today was a fistful of errors.

They handed in their papers and left the room.

'Wasn't it awful?' Anna asked.

Lindy didn't answer. She walked down the corridor in silence, sulking. What have I done now? Anna wondered. She decided not to ask. But this didn't please Lindy either.

'If you don't want to be friends any more, you've only to say so,' she announced. 'And don't sigh like that, it's very irritating.'

'You know I want to be friends.'

'I thought so once. Now I'm not so certain. Friends usually stick up for each other. I mean, you don't expect your best friend to stab you in the back, do you?'

'When am I supposed to have done that?' Anna asked, astonished.

'You're always taking sides against me.'

'Like when?'

'Like yesterday. When I was arguing with Jeremy. You said he was right.'

'But he was right,' Anna said, trying not to laugh. 'New York isn't the capital of America. Washington is.'

'Personally, I put friendship way above geography,' Lindy said absurdly. 'I suppose you think you never make mistakes. You think you're so wonderful, don't you? Just because you've got a boyfriend.'

'I haven't.'

'You don't have to lie. I don't mind your having a boyfriend. I mean, I think you're a bit young but that's your business. It's just that I think you might've told me. Friends aren't supposed to have secrets from each other.'

'Lindy, I haven't got a boyfriend,' Anna said.

'You were seen with him. Twice. In the Bluebell Café.'

Peter Elkin! Poor little Peter Elkin, whose silver heart she wore on a chain round her neck, who was like the younger brother she'd never had. She'd treated him to hot chocolate once and an ice-cream sundae once in the café on the corner of her road. Her boyfriend!

Anna burst out laughing, which was a mistake. Lindy's face went crimson and she looked at Anna with such hatred that Anna was taken aback. Before she could explain, they'd reached the entrance hall, and Miss Chivers, their music teacher, came up to talk to Lindy about the school concert. Anna walked on a little way, and waited.

A group of boys were standing in front of the table which held the pottery display. She gazed at them idly. There was an air of excitement about them that didn't go with simple admirers of pottery. They looked like people waiting for something to happen.

One of them, a tall boy with a thin, sallow face, turned round and caught Anna staring. He said something to the others, who all turned and looked at her. Then they held up their left hands in an odd sort of salute.

Surprised, she smiled and raised her own left hand in reply.

But they were not looking at her any longer. They were gazing past her to where Miss Chivers was standing with her back towards them, still talking to Lindy.

The tall boy picked up a blue vase from the table. Immediately, they began backing away, silently and swiftly, as if following a pre-arranged plan. All except one. A small, fair-haired boy, taken by surprise, was left on his own. He looked round with a bewildered smile. Anna saw that it was Peter Elkin.

The tall boy threw the vase at him.

It hit the ground at Peter's feet and shattered. When Miss Chivers turned round, she saw him standing over the broken fragments, alone. The other boys were metres away by the school notice-board.

'Now what have you done, Peter Elkin?' she demanded. She was a big woman, with a deep, resonant voice, who sounded fierce without meaning to. She could never understand why the younger children were frightened of her. Peter looked terrified.

'It wasn't him!' Anna cried. 'He didn't do it!'

'Yes, he did,' the tall boy said, scowling at her.

'Oo, you liar! You did it yourself! I saw you!'

There was an odd sound, as if the world had drawn in its breath. Everyone was staring at her. Except Miss Chivers who was beckoning to the tall boy.

'You there!' she said. 'Yes, you. Mark Bolan, isn't it? Come here.'

He left his friends and came towards them, staring at Anna. He looked astonished, as if he couldn't believe she had given him away. And then he smiled as if he'd just seen a silver lining that quite outweighed the cloud he was under.

'Now what's all this?' Miss Chivers asked. 'Did you break the vase, Mark?'

'It was an accident, miss. It slipped through my fingers.'

'So you thought you'd let a younger boy take the blame?'

Anna moved away, not wanting to listen to the boy being told off. He looked a mean sort of boy. No point in annoying him further.

'Let's go,' she whispered to Lindy.

Lindy didn't move. There was an odd look on her face. A sort of gloomy pleasure.

'You've done it now,' she said.

'I couldn't let him blame Peter. I saw him break it. He did it on purpose.'

'God, you're dumb. You've stepped right into it. I can't get you out of this.'

'What do you mean. Out of what?'

'Listen.'

At first Anna did not know what Lindy meant. Miss Chivers was standing over Mark, who was kneeling at her feet with a dustpan and brush, sweeping up the broken china. Every now and then, she pointed a commanding finger and said, 'And there's another bit.' Apart from this, the only sound was the drumming of rain on the glass roof.

What glass roof? And what rain, come to that?

Sunlight was streaming through the open door, and above her head was an ordinary plaster ceiling. The drumming sound was coming from the group of boys by the notice-board. Their fists were clenched and they were knocking their knuckles together, bone upon bone. It was not a loud sound, but it frightened Anna. She knew what it meant. Somebody had broken a rule of the Som. Somebody was going to be in trouble. Guess who?

'Let's get out of here quick,' she whispered to Lindy.

It was too late. Miss Chivers had gone, and the boys were between her and the door. They came towards her – and Lindy stepped aside.

'You betrayed me,' the tall boy said.

'Sorry. I didn't know you were one of us.'

'Don't lie. We showed you. We showed you our colour,' he said, and they all held up their left hands again in what she'd taken for a salute. Now, too late, she noticed the thin yellowish rubber band on every wrist. 'I'll have to report you,' the boy said, not attempting to hide his glee.

'That's not fair! I didn't see – I didn't think – '

'Stupidity is no excuse,' he said coldly, and some of the others smirked. Anna looked at Peter but he was looking down at his feet.

The tall boy noticed her glance.

'Peter didn't want you to interfere,' he said. 'Did you, Peter?'

'No,' he whispered, almost inaudibly, not looking up.

'Speak up,' the tall boy ordered. 'You didn't want her to interfere, did you?'

'No.'

'He's one of us. He's in the Yellows. He doesn't need a nanny. He doesn't even like you, do you, Peter?'

Peter was silent.

'Do you?' Mark Bolan repeated threateningly, putting his hand on Peter's shoulder and digging in his fingers.

'No,' Peter whispered.

'Leave him alone!' Anna cried furiously. 'I don't care if he likes me or not. And as for you, I'm glad I told. You stinking, greasy bully, I'm glad!'

The boys began knocking their knuckles together again, faster and faster.

She pushed past them and went over to Lindy, who had been standing and watching.

'They're going to report me,' she said, shrugging, trying to pretend she didn't care. 'Mean pigs.'

'They have to,' Lindy said. Her eyes were big with

the importance of Anna's crime. 'Betrayal, it couldn't be much worse. After the oath of secrecy, loyalty is the most important rule. Betray one and you betray all. They have to report you. You're in dead trouble now.'

'What can they do. I'm not in the Yellows any longer.' She smiled. 'And you won't be hard on me, will you, Lindy?'

There was no answering smile on Lindy's face.

'It's out of my hands,' she said. 'It'll be for the full council to decide and you've got enemies there. I did warn you, Anna. I told you right at the beginning it could be dangerous. It's not a game. It might have been once, but it's changed. You haven't been there much recently. They didn't say anything but they noticed. They've had their eyes on you. They never wanted you to join, but now you're in it, they can't let you go. And they can't let you get away with breaking the oath of loyalty. It's too important to them. You'll have to be punished. They'll make an example of you.'

Anna was silent. They crossed the hall and went out into the bright sunlight. Most people had already gone home, but a few boys stood, as if waiting. As soon as they saw her, they began knocking their knuckles together.

She walked out of the school gates with the sound of the muted, insistent drumming in her ears. When they reached Lindy's corner, she said, 'Come to tea, Lindy. Please.'

'I can't. Promised Mum I'd be back.'

'What shall we do this evening?'

'I've got to go out tonight. Didn't I tell you?'

'No,' Anna said. 'You didn't.'

'There's a meeting of the inner council. I'm sure I told you.'

'No,' Anna said. She stood in the sunlight, looking at her very best friend. 'You're not going to stand by me, are you, Lindy?' she asked slowly. Then she turned and ran home.

14

Ten days later, in the first week of the summer holidays, a boy walked across the road to the wool shop. It was Thursday afternoon and the sign hanging inside the glass door said: CLOSED. The boy put his nose to the glass and peered into the shadows of the shop. Then he walked on and stared through the window, past a grey cardigan and a crocheted cotton top. He nodded, as if confirming something in his mind.

On the other side of the shop, there was a green-painted front door. He went up to it, rang the bell and waited.

Nothing happened.

He rang again, and stepping back, looked up at the windows above the shop. Someone ducked back behind the curtain. He put his finger on the bell and kept it there.

Above the muffled ringing, he heard footsteps clatter down the stairs. They came towards the front door and stopped. He took his finger off the bell. For a moment there was silence, as if the person on the other side of the door was holding her breath, hoping he would go away. Then there was a scratching sound. The letterbox flap was lifted from the inside, and he saw a pair of fierce brown eyes in a shadowy slice of face.

'Who are you?' a voice demanded.

'A friend.'

'I haven't any friends. Go away.'

The flap snapped shut. The boy put his finger on the bell again.

After a moment, the door opened a cautious few centimetres. Anna Cotman looked out. The boy tried to push the door wider but it was held by a chain.

'Go away,' Anna said. 'Or I'll call the police.'

'Now that's ingratitude,' the boy said, looking hurt. 'Here I come, offering you friendship and support, kindness and comfort, and what do you do? Snarl at me. Threaten me. I don't call that nice.'

'What do you want?'

'You don't remember me, do you? You did once. In fact, you were the only person who could tell me apart from a dozen other boys. Even my father sometimes got confused. "I remember you," you said, and changed my life. I began to believe in myself. Fame and fortune seemed within my grasp. And now you've forgotten me. Ah well. *C'est la vie.*'

'Tom! Tom Smith!'

'In person. Can I come in? Or do you want us to continue talking through this chink like Pyramus and Thisbe?'

'Who?' she asked blankly, but went on before he could tell her: 'You've changed. You're much taller. And your hair's darker. And you're more – more – '

102

'Sophisticated?' he suggested hopefully. 'That's the word you're looking for, isn't it? Or wonderful?'

She smiled, but it was not much of a smile. Her expression, even now she knew who he was, was guarded. She was thinner and there were shadows under her eyes. Her soft, bright, trusting look had gone.

'You've changed, too,' he said. 'You don't look like my Annie any more.'

'I never was your Anna.'

'Annie, not Anna. Annie was a pet rabbit I once had. You used to remind me of her. I don't know why. You don't twitch your nose, do you?'

She shook her head. 'What happened to her? No, don't tell me. I expect it was something horrid.'

'I lost her. I've no proof but I've always suspected Lindy let her out of her hutch. For revenge. She was cross with me about something – I can't remember what. Lindy was always a great one for revenge. You had to be careful not to offend her or you'd find your favourite pen broken, or pages torn out of the book you were reading, or salt in your lemonade. Of course, she was younger then. She may have grown out of it by now, though I doubt it. What did you do to offend her?'

Anna was silent.

He didn't repeat his question, but told her instead that he had a message for her.

'You've come from the Som, haven't you?' she said bitterly. 'I knew you had. I wasn't taken in –'

'I haven't been taken in either,' he said plaintively. 'Here I am, left out on your doorstep like an empty milk bottle. That's no way to treat me. No, don't shut the door, Anna. I am your friend. It's official. The Goldmaster has appointed me your friend and defender. You know, for your trial.'

'Why you?'

'No one else volunteered,' he told her.

She let him in. Not because she trusted him – she trusted nobody – but because she was curious. She hadn't seen anyone from school since the end of term, not to speak to, that is. Lindy had snubbed all the girls who'd tried to make friends with Anna, and now they no longer bothered. She couldn't blame them for that. But Lindy herself hadn't been near her, and when Anna called at her house, she was told that Lindy was out or was in the bath, or having her piano lesson.

'I'll wait for her,' she had said once, but Mrs King had said vaguely: 'No, I don't think so, my dear. She may be a very long time.' And shut the door.

Anna was too proud to call again. She had no friends now, only enemies.

Often, as she walked through the streets of Redmarsh, she would hear the soft, relentless drumming, and turning round, would see a cluster of boys knocking their clenched fists together, watching her. She took to walking only in the busy streets, where the noise of traffic and the clatter and chatter of people drowned them out.

Then the notes started. She found them everywhere. At the bottom of her basket in the supermarket when she was shopping for Gran, she'd see a folded piece of paper with her name written on it in capital letters. In a crowd, she'd feel a hand in her pocket, slipping away before she had time to catch it, leaving a note behind. Pushed through the letterbox, stuck on railings, pinned to trees on the common, folded into darts and skimming through the air, they came from all directions. And they all said the same thing. Openly. Scorning to use the code she'd been so proud of.

A.C. YOUR TRIAL IS ON 21 JULY AT 5 P.M. BE THERE OR WE'LL COME FOR YOU. S.O.M.

She did not answer them. Then boys started jostling her in the streets. Sharp elbows would nudge her. Gangs of boys would run round her, yapping like dogs, flaunting the coloured bands on their wrists. Hands would slap her back, leaving coloured stickers on her shirt, until she felt like a tree marked for felling or a lamb for slaughter. And passers-by would smile and walk on, taking it for a childish game.

'You don't look well, dear,' Gran had said that morning. 'Have you got a headache?'

'No. I'm all right.'

'You're sure?'

'Yes. Don't fuss.'

Anna no longer even thought of telling her grandmother. She felt cut off, as if she were enclosed in a glass prison.

Gran, sitting in the wool shop, knitting and chatting to customers about plains and purls and patterns, seemed to belong in a different, happier world. Finding the dandelions strewn over their doorstep, she had said Anna must have a secret admirer and teased her about it. Anna knew they were a threat. 'I am the Lord of the Yellow,' he had said. 'I wouldn't try and cross me, Birdie. I really wouldn't.'

She took Tom up to the sitting-room above the shop.

'Gran's out,' she said.

'Yes, I know. They told me. She goes to Yoga on Thursday afternoons, they said. You can go then. They're very efficient, I must say.'

'Gran may be out,' Anna said sharply. 'But the Perrimens aren't. They're next door. Through there. And it's a very thin wall.'

'You mean they'd hear you if you screamed?' he said, staring at her in disbelief. 'Anna, this is me. Tom Smith. Not the local rapist. What's happened to you? Why are you so frightened? I can't understand it. I go away for a year and everything's changed when I come back. You. Jeremy. I didn't expect the red carpet treatment, but I did think somebody would welcome me a little. Offer me coffee. Ask to see my photos of the Eiffel Tower. You don't want to see them, I suppose? No. I thought not. Nobody does. All they can talk about is the trial of Anna Cotman.'

'Oh.'

'Got yourself in a mess, haven't you?'

'Did they tell you what I did?'

'Broke some silly rule,' he said, shrugging. 'To hear them talk, you'd think it was a hanging matter. Funny. I'd forgotten all about the Som. It seems like something from way back in my childhood. I wouldn't have expected it to have lasted so long.'

'Have you been to the Hall of Secrets?' she asked.

'Did you see all the new lords? And the new companions? Did they let you have a key to the storeroom?'

They had not wanted to let him in at all, he told her. He had gone, looking for Jeremy, only to be stopped at the front door by some kids, armed with sticks. Playing soldiers. Asking him for the password. He'd tried to brush them away with a joke, but they wouldn't go. For a moment, he'd almost thought they were going to attack him.

'So I said grandly, "Take me to your leader. One of you run ahead and tell him Tom Smith is home." In the end, they let me in, and there was Jeremy dressed up in his golden face and purple robe, fancying himself a king on a throne and looking a right ass. And a lot of new lords around him, who sounded too old to be playing games.'

'Was he pleased to see you?'

'He didn't stand up and cheer,' Tom said, 'but perhaps I'm being over-sensitive. He may have been beaming with joy behind his mask. But somehow I don't think so. He kept whispering and giggling with the new lords in a rather off-putting way. I thought – perhaps it isn't Jeremy at all. Perhaps some other boy has put on the golden mask. I wanted to snatch it off his face. Do you know what really shook me?'

'What?'

'I wanted it for myself. Just for a moment. As if it were a crown or something. . . . Me. Tom Smith. A sane and sensible person who believes in democracy. I actually wanted to prance around in a golden mask being king of the castle! I'm ashamed of myself.'

'I'd have liked to have been a Silver Lady,' Anna

107

confessed wistfully. 'But there's no chance of that now. I've done for myself.'

'Tell me about it,' he said gently.

She looked at his nice, ordinary face. He'd always stood up for her before. Perhaps she could trust him. She had to trust someone.

'Tom, I'm frightened,' she said. 'They're out to get me, and I don't really know why. I mean, it's not just what I've done. There's something behind it. I don't know what.'

15

'There's no hope of getting the trial cancelled,' Tom said. 'Everyone's looking forward to it too much.'

He and Anna were walking along the path by the river. It was a hot, sunless day. The sky was masked by a yellow haze and the water looked brown and dull. Only an occasional floating leaf showed the current moving slowly towards the distant sea. Then a solitary canoeist, shiny with sweat, ruffled the smooth surface, spreading a tail of silvered ripples as he passed by.

'It's quite outshone the games in popularity,' Tom went on. 'They must've been getting tired of all that bouncing about. Too like school sports. Much nicer to sit and watch someone else in the dock. Makes them feel safe and smug. And a public punishment — wow! I bet they'd love to see you hanged. Nothing personal, mind,' he added smiling at her. 'It's just because they're bored.'

'So what shall I do?' Anna asked, and thought of foolish things like stowing away on a ship bound for the other side of the world. Dear Gran, don't worry about me. I'll be all right, love Anna. Poor Gran, who did love Anna, having no other family to love. Of course she would worry.

'Don't look so depressed,' Tom said. 'Haven't you any faith in your appointed defender? I rather fancy myself as a barrister. Don't you think a wig would suit me?'

'It'd look stupid above a mask.'

'I'm not going to wear one,' he told her. 'Faces are masks enough, without hiding behind a bit of painted paper. And you're not to, either. You and I will be the only real people there.'

He seemed very cheerful today. Yesterday, when he'd heard all she had to say, he'd frowned. 'God, I hope it isn't – ' he'd begun, and then broken off, muttering to himself: 'Surely Jeremy wouldn't be such a fool.'

'Isn't what? What do you mean?' she'd asked.

He had shaken his head and refused to tell her.

Normally, it would have annoyed her, this shutting her out as if she were still a small child from whom things had to be hidden. She was not a fool. She knew there were ugly, evil things in the world.

But he was Jeremy's friend. His first loyalty belonged to Jeremy and not to her. She couldn't blame him for that. Jeremy with his bright hair and his face, which even when unmasked, still glowed as if the gold paint had permeated his skin. She remembered how he had smiled at her in the churchyard when she had said she would be constant, come wind, come weather. What must he think of her now, the disgraced companion who had broken the rule of loyalty? She sighed.

A group of boys were coming along the path towards them. Boys from their school. As they came near, they began knocking their knuckles together. Anna put her tongue out defiantly.

'Stop doing that or I'll bang your heads together,' Tom said.

'She's a traitor,' one of the boys muttered. 'We got the right.'

'Have you indeed? People are innocent until they're proven guilty. Didn't you know that?'

'She was seen. There were witnesses. Lots of them. Tony here was there when she done it. Weren't you, Tone!'

'Yes.' The boy addressed nodded vigorously. He was a small, pink-faced boy with large round spectacles. 'I saw her. I heard her. She pointed Mark out in front of our noses. We got the right to drum her.'

But they were only first-formers. When Tom took a threatening step towards them, they fled down the path, only stopping to jeer when they were well out of reach.

'Traitor! Traitor!' they shrieked, and a duck on the brown water turned its head to stare.

'Shall I chase them?' Tom asked.

Anna shook her head. 'It's too hot. Besides, they're right. I did betray Mark Bolan. I suppose I am a traitor, but it didn't seem like that. I only told the truth. It's not as if Mark got into any trouble. She shouted at him a bit. You know Miss Chivers, she's got a loud voice but she never does anything. And he's tough. It'd take more than that to make him cry.'

She thought of Peter with his pale nervous face too often wet with tears. He had betrayed their friendship but she didn't hate him for it. He was weak. He couldn't help it. Funny. Mark Bolan would probably make a more loyal friend but she didn't like him.

'We've got to talk,' Tom said. 'Let's sit down somewhere.'

'What about over there in the long grass?'

'It'll be full of lovers and spies and spiders. No, we'll sit in the open where we can see our enemies coming. We've got to plan our strategy.'

He's enjoying himself, Anna thought. Everybody's going to have a fine time at the trial except me.

They sat down on the bank beside the river. Anna took her shoes off and dangled her feet in the water. It was cool and muddy. On the opposite bank, a man sat fishing.

'You're to be judged by the full council of the lords,' Tom told her. 'If you plead guilty, it'll be over quickly. All they'll have to do is decide on your punishment.'

'I don't want to be punished.'

'Who does? You'll just have to be a brave bunny rabbit. After all, they can't kill you.'

That's what she kept telling herself when she woke in the night. They can't kill me, she'd tell the moon as it looked through her window. They probably won't even hurt me much.

But fears as old as time stirred in the mud at the bottom of her mind — chanting and firelight and shadows on the wall. The sound of screaming in a dark cave.

Make me brave, God, she prayed. And lying awake in the night, she'd chant softly the words of her favourite hymn.

'Hobgoblin nor foul fiend
Can daunt my spirit. . . .'

She couldn't tell Tom about these dark fancies. He'd laugh at her.

'I don't trust the Lord of the Yellow,' she said.

'Can't say I care for him myself,' Tom agreed. 'Tell me, how many friends have you among the other lords?'

'You,' she said.

'Only me?' He looked startled.

She flushed. 'I haven't seen much of the others recently. They come at different times. You know, practising for the games with their companions. They used to tease me in the old days, before the new lords came and things changed.'

'So they did. But they liked you. I remember that. They said you were a nice kid.'

'Did they?' She was pleased.

'You can't count on Lindy, I'm afraid. No one can. She picks people up and drops them like empty sweet wrappers when she's finished with them.'

'Don't say that. She's my friend. Or was.'

Tom looked at her and smiled. 'And you're the girl they say broke the rule of loyalty.'

They were silent for a moment. Anna wriggled her toes in the water and tried to catch a floating twig. The solitary canoeist was coming back, more slowly now the current was against him and he was tired.

'Not guilty, that's what we'll go for,' Tom said. 'Let's give them a run for their money. They'll like us better for putting on a show. Let's see. We know the four new lords are against us. The Goldmaster? I'm afraid he'll go along with them. Lindy? Who knows? Perhaps I'm hard on her. It can't have been easy for her. She was always such a sharp, plain little thing and there was Jeremy, everybody's picture of an eighteen-carat solid-gold hero. No wonder she went sour. Nobody took any notice of her when he was around, yet she's much the cleverer. Life isn't fair.'

Perhaps that's why Lindy's turned against me, Anna thought. Not because of Peter Elkin but because of Jeremy. She must've noticed the way I gazed at him when he was wearing his golden mask. I couldn't help it. I was dazzled.

'Do you think she'll vote against me?' she asked.

'She might – ' he broke off and laughed. 'Not if Jeremy does. They've quarrelled. They'll cancel each other out. Good. I'll only have to win the old lords over and we'll be. . . . Let me see. Five against and five for you. What happens then, petit lapin? God knows. Will they let the companions vote? We can't have that. They're a bloodthirsty lot.' He caught sight of her anxious face and said quickly, 'Don't look so worried. I'll think of something. I'll get you out of this mess, I promise, even if I have to bribe the jury.'

He walked her back to the wool shop and accepted Mrs Cotman's invitation to supper. After supper, he showed them his photographs of Paris. There were only three of the Eiffel Tower, and in two of them it was in the background, pointing up at the sky behind a pretty girl.

'Who's that?' Anna asked.

'Claudine. The landlady's daughter.'

'She looks nice.'

'She is. She's a teacher.'

'Oh, she's quite old then,' Anna said, and flushed when they both laughed. She'd sounded jealous, but she wasn't. She wasn't in love with Tom or anybody. Not even Jeremy. The Goldmaster did not really exist. He was only a golden dream in a dark building.

16

On the day before the trial, the weather changed. Clouds scurried across the sky, chased by a nipping wind. Anna felt restless. She didn't want to go out. She didn't want to stay in.

'I think I'll go up to the shopping centre at Marsh Cross,' she said. 'Is there anything you want, Gran?'

'Don't think so, dear,' Mrs Cotman said. 'I should take a coat. It's much colder. Is Lindy going with you?'

'Not today.'

Nor ever again, by the look of it. 'Try to make it up with Lindy,' Tom had advised.

'I did try.'

'Try again.'

So she did, but it was no good. Mrs King was beginning to frown with embarrassment when she saw it was Anna again at the door. Who is that knocking? A beggar?

Gran had noticed, of course. 'You haven't quarrelled with Lindy, have you?' she asked.

'Me? With Lindy?' Anna repeated, as if astonished at the thought. 'I was round at her house only yesterday. And the day before.'

Trick-truth, Lindy used to call this sort of answer. She'd scolded Anna about it in the days when they were still friends. God, she claimed, preferred a good, honest lie.

'Practise in front of a mirror until you can tell a whopper without blushing,' she said. 'That's what I did. I'd look myself in the eye and say out loud, "I'm as pretty as my mum." It's a wonder the mirror didn't crack.' Then she'd glanced sideways at Anna, daring her to say the wrong thing.

But Anna had opened her eyes wide and said boldly, 'You are far, far prettier than your mum, Lindy. There. Is that what you meant by a good, honest lie?' and Lindy had laughed.

I do like her, Anna thought. I know she's bossy and sly and as sharp as a monkey puzzle tree, but we had fun together. When she was in a good mood, she made the other girls seem as dull as bread and butter.

The shopping centre at Marsh Cross was crowded with strangers. No one looked at Anna coldly. No boys drummed their knuckles at her. She walked slowly along, looking in all the bright windows, but not stopping until she reached Frankton's. There, on the jewellery counter, was a shallow box containing lucky charms, each fastened to a small velvet square. Silver charms to wear on a silver bracelet; tiny boots and top hats, hearts and horseshoes. . . . No silver birds. Her luck was out. Here was one shaped like a mask, the mask of comedy. She picked it up. The Silver Lady grinned up at her with empty eyes. What sort of luck would that bring her? Good or bad? She held it in her hand, undecided.

There was a man standing further along the counter, a short, middle-aged man with a square face. He did not seem interested in the coloured beads on the stand in front of him. He wasn't even looking at them. His head was turned towards her.

'I can't make up my mind,' she said, putting the silver mask back in the tray, wondering if he was a store detective, standing there so quiet and intent. But if he was, it was not her he was interested in.

'It is difficult to choose,' he agreed politely, but his pale blue eyes were still watching something over her left shoulder.

She turned.

There were three people behind her. A fat woman in a green dress, a man with a baby in a pushchair, and Peter Elkin.

Peter was standing in front of a display of cigarette lighters. His back was turned towards her but there was no mistaking the pale hair hanging in limp wisps over the thin neck, or the protective hunch of the narrow shoulders. She knew at once he was the one the man was watching. If he'd been starring in a film called 'The Young Thief', he couldn't have acted more suspiciously. The way he sidled up to the stand, the quick nervous glances he gave – upwards to check the large angled mirrors suspended from the ceiling, then right and left but never far enough round to spot Anna and the store detective. (She was sure now that he was a detective. His eyes were so watchful, so patient and so cold.)

118

Before Anna could decide what to do, it was too late. Peter's hand reached out, took something from the stand that glinted gold, and put it in his pocket. Then he turned to go.

Anna and the detective moved forwards at the same time and collided.

'Ow!' Anna cried loudly, clutching the man's arm with both hands, and holding on tightly. 'My foot! You've hurt my foot! It's broken!'

Peter looked round, one quick terrified glance, and fled out of the store.

The man pulled his arm out of Anna's grip, bumped into the fat woman in the green dress, rebounded off the full curve of her stomach, tripped over a baby's pushchair and fell down on the floor. It was definitely not his lucky day. By the time he had picked himself up, Anna had gone after Peter.

He could be anywhere. So many shops, cafés, boutiques. He might be trying on clothes in a cubicle or locked in a toilet. No. Not Peter. He wouldn't have the courage to stay in the shopping centre. He'd bolt for the nearest exit.

Then what? Marsh Cross was an island in a roaring sea of traffic. A tangled knot of fast roads surrounded it, over-passes and under-passes – no place for a pedestrian to venture. There were narrow pavements but nobody ever walked on them. He'd be as conspicious as a fly on a spider's web. Safer to wait for a bus.

That was where she found him, standing in the queue for the 210B for Redmarsh. The collar of his denim jacket was turned up, his shoulders hunched and his eyes shut. If there'd been a bucket of sand available, he'd have buried his head in it. But at least, she thought, he'd had the nerve to stop running.

'It's going to rain,' she said, coming up and grasping his arm. 'Put this over your head.' With her free hand, she took off her nylon scarf and held it out. He had jumped violently and now gazed at her in terror, making no move to take it.

'Stand still,' she commanded, and arranging the bright green scarf over his head, tied it under his chin. No one paid any attention to them. 'There,' she whispered. 'You look like a girl now. You'll be safe.'

He didn't say anything. She was holding his arm again and she could feel him trembling. He was still shaking when the bus came.

They sat side by side on the back seat. The bus was not crowded. There was nobody on the seat in front of them. It was safe to talk, if they whispered.

Anna could hear Peter's breath whistling in his throat. He had taken off the green headscarf, but his face still had a greenish pallor. She was afraid he was going to faint. But as the bus left Marsh Cross and turned into the quieter streets of Stokes Green, he seemed to relax. Without looking at her, he mumbled, 'Thanks.'

'Give it to me,' she whispered fiercely, holding out her hand.

'I did,' he said, thinking she meant the scarf. 'You put it in your pocket.'

'Not that. It. The thing you stole.'

Slowly he put his hand in his pocket and brought it out. It was a gold-coloured cigarette lighter, with a small blue stone in the centre of each side. She held it in the palm of her hand.

'You could've been caught,' she whispered angrily. 'You would've been. There was a store detective watching you. He'd have got you if I hadn't stopped him. He'll remember me. I'll never be able to go to Marsh Cross again. He'll think I was in on it. And you! You risked getting a police record for this. This cheap rubbishy thing. You didn't think it was real gold, did you? Look, the stuff's wearing off already. And those are not sapphires, they're blue glass.'

He was crying silently, tears running down his cheeks and dripping on to his denim jacket.

'What did you do it for?' she asked. 'It doesn't seem like you. I thought you were honest.'

'It was my task,' he whispered.

'Your *task*?' She stared at him, hardly able to believe her ears, 'You mean, for the Yellow Lord? For the Som?'

'Don't tell them I told you. They'll kill me.'

'Is this the first time?' she asked. 'How many tasks have you done?'

'This is my fourth,' he whispered, so faintly that she could hardly hear him.

'You mean you've been told to steal things? Four times?'

'It's not stealing,' he said quickly. 'We don't keep the things we take. We have to give them to our lord, and he puts them back – '

'And you really believe that?' Anna asked scornfully. Peter flushed and was silent.

'What have you stolen for him before?' she asked.

'A penknife from Woolworth's and a leather wallet from the market. Cigarettes. They send someone with you the first time to watch. One of the companions cheated, you see. He bought a key-ring and pretended he'd nicked it. He had to be punished. But after you've stolen two things, they trust you by yourself – '

'They trust you, do they?' Anna said dryly and he bit his lip. 'So he tells you what to take?'

'Yes. He wanted a gold lighter this time,' he told her, and looked wistfully at the lighter in her hand, as if longing to ask for it back, but not quite daring to. 'Are you sure it isn't gold?'

'Positive.'

'It wouldn't have done, then,' he said sadly.

'Will he be angry if you don't bring anything back?'

'Yes.'

She was suddenly furious. She wanted to hit the Lord of the Yellow, scream at him, tear the yellow mask from his face and spit in his eye. But he wasn't there. There was only the silly little drip on the seat next to her, crying again.

'You're so wet,' she said crossly.

'I'm sorry.'

'That little silver heart you gave me,' she asked. 'Was it stolen, too?

'No! No, it wasn't, honestly,' he protested. 'I bought it. I saved up my pocket money. I did!' He looked anxiously at her face, and then added dismally, 'It wasn't worth much.'

'No,' Anna agreed, knowing he wasn't talking about the price. 'It wasn't, was it?'

They travelled on in silence. Anna played with the lighter in her hand and wondered what to do with it. Throw it away? Post it back to the store? Show it to Tom?

'Would it help you to tell them about it?' Peter asked suddenly. His face had a desperate look, as if he'd screwed up his courage so tight that it hurt. 'At the trial, I mean? You can tell them if you like. I don't mind. I want you to. I didn't mean it – what I said. You know, about not liking you. I didn't mean it.'

'I know you didn't, Peter.'

'Only I was so frightened – it's the Yellow Lord. I hate him!'

'But if I tell, he'll know I must've got it from someone. Won't he guess it was you? Won't you get into trouble?'

'I don't care. I won't be there. I'm not going to the trial. They'd only make me say things against you. I'm not brave. I can't stand up to them. So I'm going to bed,' he said and smiled. 'I've made up my mind. I'm going to be ill.'

'You can't be ill for ever,' she pointed out.

'Yes, I can,' he said stubbornly. 'If they try and make me get up, I shall scream and scream and scream until I make myself really ill. I've done it before. People are nicer to me when I'm ill. Except you. You've always been kind. You're good. That's why the Lord of the Yellow hates you so much, because he's evil and you're good.'

'I'm not,' Anna protested, laughing and embarrassed, glad Lindy wasn't there to hear him.

'Yes, you are,' he said, but he said it gloomily, as if he didn't think that the right side would win.

17

Anna woke from a nightmare, sitting bolt upright in bed, staring around in terror. But there was only her familiar room; the grey oblong of her window, the dim shapes of her furniture against the walls. It was an in-between time, neither properly night nor day.

She was afraid to go back to sleep in case her nightmare was waiting for her, so she switched on her light and tried to read. But the print kept dancing before her tired eyes, and when she blinked and looked away, she seemed to see shadowy words printed in the air – 'Be there or we'll come for you.'

'I said I'll be there,' she cried to the empty room. 'Tomorrow – no, it's already today. Today is the day of my trial.'

It was raining when she woke again, a misty drizzling rain that looked as if it might go on for ever.

'Not a very cheerful day for you,' her grandmother said at breakfast. 'Good for trade, though. Makes people think of knitting cardigans and scarves. What time are you going to Lindy's?'

'This afternoon. I won't be in to supper. We're

having – a sort of party,' Anna said, and thought, I mustn't cry. Whatever happens, I'm not going to cry.

'Is it somebody's birthday?' Gran asked, smiling.

'No. Just a party. I won't be late. And anyway, Tom said he'd bring me safe home.'

'Tom Smith?' Mrs Cotman said and raised her eyebrows.

They sat in silence, wrapped in their separate thoughts. Mrs Cotman was thinking that she didn't want Anna to grow up too quickly. Anna was not yet fourteen. Too young for boyfriends, especially older boys like this Tom Smith, with his smiles and his photographs of the Eiffel Tower.

Anna was thinking of the trial, trying to make herself brave. Her lips moved soundlessly – 'Hobgoblin nor foul fiend, Can daunt my spirit. . . .' They're only a pack of stupid boys, stupid boys in fancy dress. I'm not scared of them.

It was difficult not to let her courage leak away as the grey hours crept by. She was glad when it was time to go and meet Tom at the Bluebell Café. 'I'll treat you to a cream tea,' he'd said. 'And we'll make our final plans.'

She got there early and, choosing a table by the window, sat looking out. It had stopped raining, though the pavements were still wet. She saw Tom at the other end of the street. There were three boys behind him. They crossed the road when he did. They stopped when he did. He turned and said something to them. Then he came on alone.

The door opened and he walked in, smiling cheerfully. Judas, she thought.

'Who are those boys?' she demanded.

'Oh, them,' he said, glancing at the window. 'I was hoping you wouldn't see them yet. Don't look at me like that. It wasn't my fault. The lords insisted. They're afraid you won't come and think how silly they'd look, all set to be judge and jury and nobody in the dock. Those boys are your escort. They'll stay with you when I leave, and bring you to the Hall of Secrets when it's time.'

'Supposing I won't come?'

'They're to make you.'

'*How? What do you mean?*'

'Don't look so scared,' he said quickly. 'Sorry. I was only quoting the Lord of the Yellow. That lot out there are only kids. They've no more idea what he meant than I have. I suppose they might try and carry you there.'

'I wouldn't let them. I could scream.'

'Yes, you could,' he agreed. 'Do you want to? If you like, we'll both scream together. When do you want to start? Now?'

'Yes,' she said, but added quickly as he opened his mouth, 'No! Don't! You weren't really going to, were you?'

'Of course. I'm your defender. If you really think screaming is the best way to deal with this mess, then we'll scream.' He said it lightly, but then added, suddenly serious, 'You may be right, at that. If we screamed loud enough, somebody'd be bound to ask us why.'

She looked at him, puzzled and dismayed.

'You mean you don't think we can win?'

'I thought we might. I've got quite a good case. To tell the truth, I've been looking forward to putting it. Showing off – you know, listen to Tom Smith. He may not be much to look at, but, wow, isn't he clever.'

'Aren't you?'

'Not clever enough,' he said ruefully. 'I thought it was a game with rules, good old fair play and all that. But it isn't any longer. It's all changed. It's gone bad – ' He broke off as the waitress came with their cream teas. Anna looked at the scones and jam and thick yellow cream, and felt sick.

'I don't think I can eat anything,' she said when the waitress had gone.

'Try. We've got to keep our strength up whatever we decide to do. Take one bite to begin with and work up from there. One step at a time. That's what Jeremy used to say when we were kids, daring ourselves to do something dangerous. He was always reading about heroes and knights of the Round Table and Robin Hood. He went for all the big words, courage and honour, justice and mercy. God, how he's changed. How he'd sneer at them now. He listens to the new lords and just laughs when I try to be serious. I told him he'd lose his good looks if he wasn't careful, spending so much time in a dark room, drinking and smoking God-knows-what filth. It's true. Have you seen him recently without his mask? He looks sick and sweaty and – and rotten.'

Anna stared at him, appalled. 'May the mask of

bone break through my rotting flesh. . . .' But Tom was not talking about the oath of secrecy. He was talking about drugs.

'I don't know for sure,' he said hastily. 'Don't say anything to anyone. I could be utterly wrong. It's just – I've no proof, though. They say you can tell by their eyes but the light was bad and he kept blinking. I couldn't get near him.'

'I can't believe it,' Anna said.

She didn't want to believe it, not of the Goldmaster. Not of Lindy's brother. The golden boy laughing with his friends in the playground, swimming in the summer river, running and leaping down the winter streets – she couldn't bear to think of him rotting in some dark and dirty corner, sick and stupid with drugs. Not Jeremy!

'You must be wrong,' she said.

'I hope I am.'

But Tom did not think he was. He knew Jeremy. Jeremy was given to sudden enthusiasms for people, new people he could impress, not old friends who knew him too well and laughed at him. Jeremy was weak. He'd never be able to say no. The Lord of the Yellow had only to flatter him. . . . He'd tell himself it'd be all right. Just once . . . or twice. *He'd* never get hooked, not our golden boy. Oh, Jeremy, you fool! Why wasn't I there to stop it?

'What are you going to do?' Anna asked.

'What can I do?' Tom demanded angrily. 'Tell Harry? Or the police? Jeremy's my oldest friend. I can't. Supposing I'm wrong? I'm only guessing. I'd ask him straight out, but I can't get hold of him on his own. I think he's avoiding me. He's out whenever I call at his house.'

Or hiding in his room, Anna thought. Poor Mrs King, the lies she has to tell for her children.

'I had a stupid idea that I might win him over at your trial,' Tom said. 'Dreamt of making a grand speech about honour and justice and all the things he used to care about. Daft, wasn't I? Don't know who I thought I was, Superman or something. I should have known better at my age.'

But Anna was younger than he was. Her eyes shone with hope.

'It might work, Tom. Can't you try?'

'Anna, it was only a stupid dream. Besides, I was going to tell you. I've changed my mind. I don't think you should go to the trial. I think you'd better go home.'

'Why?' she asked, astonished.

'They're not going to give us a chance, Anna.'

'I don't care. I'll risk it. Please, Tom, make your grand speech.'

He shook his head frowning. 'I don't like it. I don't want you there.'

'What about those boys?' she asked, jerking her thumb at the window. 'What about my escort?'

'Don't worry about them. I'll see them off.'

'And what about the next lot? And the next? All those notes I had: "Be there or we'll come for you." I don't want to live looking over my shoulder. I'd rather get it over. Besides,' she added, smiling, 'if I don't, a friend of mine is going to have to stay in bed for ever.'

She told him about the tasks the Lord of the Yellow had set his companions, the band of little thieves he had trained to bring him whatever he fancied.

'Will it help?' she asked.

'It might. It might be just the thing. Why didn't you tell me sooner? I must go and see Peter Elkin – '

'I didn't say it was Peter!'

'Anna, I hadn't been back two days before I heard you'd set yourself up as champion of a poor little weed called Peter Elkin. Who else could have told you?'

'You mustn't try and make him come. He'd only be ill.'

'All I want is a letter from him. I won't bully him, I promise. If he doesn't want to let me have one, we'll manage without. OK? Now, if we're going ahead with it, there's some silly rigamarole I'm supposed to teach you, then I must be off.'

When Tom had gone, Anna watched him through the window. It was raining again. As soon as he was out of sight, the three boys came into the café. They sat at the table next to hers, ordered three cokes and paid for them when they came.

'We might have to leave in a hurry,' one of them told the waitress.

Anna smiled at them and they stared back disapprovingly. The only time they took their eyes off her was when they looked at the clock on the wall.

18

The blindfold had not been put on very well. Looking down, Anna could see the shadow of her own nose and a slice of doorstep. Did they really imagine she wouldn't know where she was? By tilting her head back, she saw that the door to the Hall of Secrets was already open.

Careful. Somebody was watching her. She could see the toes of his shoes.

She knocked three times on the ground with the rod she had been given. Nothing happened. The watcher within did not move.

Behind her, one of the three boys snuffled and cleared his throat. That would be the young one who had a summer cold. A fat boy – he'd looked wistful when she'd offered them her uneaten cream tea in the café. But the leader, a boy so thin and sour that it looked as if he'd spent his life refusing food, had shaken his head violently.

'We were warned you'd try and get round us,' he said.

Would he report her for trying to corrupt them with cream scones? Probably.

'Who's that knocking?' the unseen watcher demanded suddenly.

'A beggar,' Anna replied.

'Where's your begging bowl?'

'In my heart and in my head.' What nonsense it was! She tilted her head back a little further. He was not wearing socks. His ankles were thin and grubby.

'Who put on this blindfold?' he demanded angrily. Her head was jerked forward and the cloth round her eyes was pulled down, blocking out the light.

'Come in, beggar,' he said, gripping her arm and digging in his nails so hard that she yelped. She was pulled forward so violently that she banged her head against the doorjamb, stumbled and hit her shoulder against some sharp corner. Hands took hold of her other arm and held her.

'Stand still!' somebody commanded.

Now she could smell candle-smoke and dust. All around her there was a faint seething, whispering sound of movement, like worms slithering through the dark. Then the drumming began, knuckle against knuckle, slowly at first, then faster and faster, and her heart kept time with it until she thought it would burst.

'Kneel down, beggar,' a new voice ordered. 'You are in the presence of the secret lords of the Som.'

Anna knelt down. The floor was gritty. No one had swept it since she left. Somehow this simple, domestic thought gave her courage. She'd been useful to them. They'd better remember that.

'What do you want, beggar?'

'Justice!' she cried, her voice ringing out loud and clear. 'I want justice!'

'Take off her blindfold.'

After the complete darkness, the candle-light dazzled her. The far end of the long room, lit like a stage, was separated from her by a host of shifting, shuffling, muttering shadows, who turned their heads to stare. Their dim faces, sliced in two by their narrow masks, were hardly recognisable as human. Their mouths grinned and whispered. She saw the blurred flutter of their hands as they drummed their fists together.

They had left an aisle down the centre of the room. At the far end, the Goldmaster sat on a throne covered by brightly coloured cloths and cushions. The hood of his purple robe was thrown back, and his golden mask and shining hair seemed brighter than the light from the candle-jars that ringed his feet.

At the table on his right, his lords sat, masked and hooded in their various colours. Each had a candle-jar beside him, and paper and pencils ready. The table on the other side was empty, except for a low stool placed on the top.

'Bring the prisoner here,' the Goldmaster said.

As she was led forward, the chanting began. 'Som – som – som – som – som – ' louder and louder until the noise boomed out like an enormous drum: 'SOM – SOM – SOM – SOM – SOM!'

She clenched her fists. I won't let them see I'm frightened. Hobgoblin nor foul fiend can daunt my spirit . . . Help me to be brave, God.

They were stamping on the floor now, their mouths opening and shutting like fish: 'SOM – SOM – SOM – SOM – SOM!'

'Why don't you stick pins in me?' she shouted bitterly, and those near enough to hear her over the din, stopped with their mouths open, startled, as if they hadn't realised she could speak.

Her escort jerked her forward.

'Keep your mouth shut, traitor,' one of them muttered.

Traitor. A companion heard the word and repeated it. It blew around the room like an ill wind, and now they were all roaring, 'Traitor! Traitor! Traitor!'

She was frightened now, her courage all run out. When the Goldmaster asked her if she accepted the justice of the court, she was confused and did not answer.

'Well?' he said impatiently. 'It's a simple enough question, surely. Do you accept the justice of this court?'

The slightest touch of kindness would have made her dissolve into tears: the contempt in his voice stung her to anger.

'What justice!' she shouted. 'I've been blindfolded, my arms pinched and pulled, my head banged against the wall! You've let them shout at me and call me traitor! You've taken away my mask and my Som name. The trial hasn't even begun yet! What sort of justice is that, Goldmaster?'

A shocked silence. Then somebody began to clap.

The noise came from the lord's table. Anna turned

her head and saw that the Silver Lady, sitting between the old lords and the new, was clapping her hands together in an ostentatious manner, holding them up high so that everyone could see.

'A good point,' she said, nodding her head so that the light danced on her silver mask. 'Yes, I must say I think that the prisoner has made a good point. The verdict should come after the trial, not before.'

Watched by everyone in the room, she picked up her pencil and drew a line down the paper in front of her, dividing it into two columns. 'For,' she said, writing it down, 'and Against.' She put a large tick in the first column and sat back. 'There!'

The Goldmaster said, his voice tight with anger:

'If you can't behave, Silver Lady, I'll have you thrown out.'

'Me? What have I done? I thought the paper was meant for us to use. Didn't you, Red?'

The Red Lord, who was sitting beside her, nodded his head.

'That was certainly my opinion,' he said. 'I thought we were supposed to keep the score. How else can we know who's won?'

'We're not meant to make up our minds already, are we?' the Blue Lord asked innocently.

'Can't be,' the White Lord said. 'The trial hasn't begun yet.'

They're on my side, Anna thought joyfully. All the old lords, and perhaps the Silver Lady – though with Lindy you could never be sure what game she was playing. Tom must've won them over. Where was he?

She looked round but could not see him anywhere.

There was only the Goldmaster in a quivering rage. The candle-light cast flickering shadows over his golden mask so that it appeared to be burning. But his voice was ice cold.

'That's enough,' he said. 'Put the prisoner in the dock.'

Anna did not want to sit on the stool on top of the second table, a target for all eyes. But she knew it was no good struggling. 'I'll walk by myself,' she said, but they would not allow her so much dignity, and dragging her to the table, lifted her up bodily and placed her on the stool. The candles below her ringed her with fire, and beyond them, she saw the glint of eyes staring. Hundreds of eyes.

Where was Tom?

19

'Let the trial begin,' the Goldmaster said. 'Herald, summon the Lord Accuser.'

A companion in a narrow red mask stepped forward and blew a long high note on a recorder. There was a rustling as the other companions sat down on the floor, and turned their faces to look at him expectantly.

'Where is the Lord Accuser?' he cried. 'Let him come forward!'

The chanting began again. The Lord of the Yellow stepped out of the shadows behind the throne. He bowed to the Goldmaster and then, turning to the audience, held up his gloved hands. The chanting died away.

He looked across to where Anna sat on her lonely eminence.

'So this is the traitor,' he said.

'No!' she whispered, but he'd turned away.

The Herald blew once more on his recorder.

'Where is the Lord Defender?'

Now a figure in a green robe strolled out from behind the throne, bowed politely to the Goldmaster, then turned to face the companions. His hood came right forwards, casting a deep shadow over his face, and they peered at him uncertainly. Then he raised his hands and pushed his hood back on to his shoulders, and they gasped. His face was bare. Unmasked.

A murmuring arose from the crowded room, like bees disturbed.

'Who is it? Why isn't he wearing a mask?' some asked and others replied: 'Dunno. Can't be a lord, not with his face showing. Funny, innit?'

'Tom,' Anna whispered, when he came up to her. 'I thought they'd locked you out. I couldn't see you anywhere. I thought I was all alone.'

'I object!' the Lord of the Yellow cried immediately. 'Goldmaster, is the accused to be allowed to chat with her defender while the court waits?'

'You had a word with her yourself,' Tom said sharply. 'You called her a traitor, as if you were judge and jury rolled into one.'

'She is a traitor.'

'Objection!' Tom cried in his turn. 'Goldmaster, he's trying to prejudice the court against this innocent girl – '

'Objection!' the Yellow Lord shouted. 'He called her innocent, which is prejudging the case and usurping the role of this court – '

'Objection! The accused is deemed innocent until proved otherwise!'

'Objection!' one of the companions muttered and several of them laughed, and took it up. 'Objection, objection!' they chanted, grinning and pushing each other.

'Silence!' the Goldmaster shouted, and they quietened immediately. 'You're giving me a headache,' he complained petulantly. 'Let's get on with it. Bring on your witnesses, Lord Accuser. Are they ready?'

'Yes, Goldmaster. But I must give my opening speech first.'

'Must you? Oh, very well, but for God's sake, keep it short,' the Goldmaster said, and leaning back against his cushions, clicked his fingers. A small blue-masked companion stepped forward and handed him a silver cup, like the ones people win for tennis or swimming. There was indeed something engraved on the side, although Anna was too far away to read what it said. He put the rim of the cup to the parted lips of his mask and tilted his head back. A thin trickle of wine ran from the corner of the golden mouth.

Then the Lord of the Yellow walked forward.

'Goldmaster, lords, lady and companions of the Som,' he said. 'All of us have taken the dread oath of secrecy. All of us have sworn to obey the rules of the Som. Didn't we give the blood of obedience at our swearing-in? Tell me, my friends, which is the most important rule?'

'The rule of loyalty!' they roared.

'The rule of loyalty. Yes. For isn't that the whole purpose of the Som? That we stand together against oppression, the strong protecting the weak? We must know that we can trust one another, can count on one another for support against our enemies. We must lie for one another, if need be. Fight for one another, if need be. Even die, if death is necessary. For aren't we all blood brothers in the Som?'

'Yes! Yes! Yes!' they roared.

He held up his hands to quieten them, then strode over to Anna.

'Look at this girl!' he cried, pointing to her quite unnecessarily, for all eyes had already turned her way. 'Oh yes, she looks innocent enough, doesn't she, with those big brown eyes and that baby face? Like somebody's little sister, you'd expect her still to be playing with dolls and kittens, wouldn't you? See how she blushes. She's going to cry, the poor little thing. *Don't be fooled by her*!' he shouted suddenly, making Anna jump. 'She's a foul, dirty traitor! She betrayed one of us. She betrayed your blood brother! Didn't you?' he cried, leaping up on to the table beside her. 'You know you're guilty. Confess it! Go on, confess and get it over with!'

She might have confessed if he hadn't looked so like the devil. The candle-jars lit his masked face from below, and grotesque shadows seemed to leap out of him and caper across the ceiling. Then Tom pulled him down from the table, and they struggled together.

The recorder sounded again, shrill and insistent. The Goldmaster, picking up a scarlet cushion from his throne, threw it so accurately that it skimmed between the two fighting lords, brushing both their faces. The Lord of the Yellow jumped back as if stung, his hands up to his face, quickly adjusting his mask.

'Come here, both of you,' the Goldmaster said coldly.

Anna could not hear what he said to them, for he kept his voice low. The companions whispered and fidgeted and stared at her. She bit her thumb to keep herself from crying.

'Call your first witness, Lord Accuser,' said the Goldmaster at last, settling back on his cushions and holding out his silver cup for the Blue Companion to refill.

'Yellow Dog! Will Yellow Dog come up? Calling Yellow Dog.'

It was Mark Bolan. He came forward with a swagger, bowed low to the Goldmaster and then to the Lord of the Yellow. A chair had been placed between the throne and Anna's table. He stood behind it, resting his hands lightly on the back, and looked at Anna with sly malice.

'Do you swear by the dread oath of the Som to tell the truth, the whole truth and nothing but the truth?'

'I do.'

'Your Som name is Yellow Dog and you are a student at the Redmarsh Comprehensive?'

'Yes, my lord.'

'I want you to tell the court what happened on the afternoon of July 13 last.'

'Certainly, my lord,' he said with relish. 'After the bell, I went with my lot to the school entrance hall. We was on a toughening-up exercise, see? It was the shrimp's turn to be toughened up. Well, you know what he's like, my lord. Feeble. A sniveller. We was afraid he'd let us down at the games. So we had to put him through it, didn't we?'

Poor Peter, poor little shrimp, Anna thought, and hoped he had stayed safe in bed.

'He'd agreed to it,' Mark Bolan said. 'We wasn't doing anything he hadn't agreed to, my lord.'

'Get on with it.'

'Yes, Goldmaster. Sorry, Goldmaster. Well, we were about to begin when we saw her staring at us – '

'Her? You mean, the accused?'

'Yes, my lord. Anna Cotman. We knew she was one of us, so we give her the sign. You know – ' He held up his left wrist and pointed to the yellow band. 'Then I broke the vase. The Shrimp had to take the blame without blubbing. That was the test, see? But she spoiled it. She went and told on me.'

'She betrayed you?'

'Yes, my lord,' Mark Bolan said with noticeable satisfaction.

'Even though you had warned her you were on Som business?'

'Yes, my lord.'

'Why? The Lord Defender, I'm sure, will ask you that. He'll try and claim she had no motive. Can you think of one? Did she have any reason to bear you a grudge?'

'No, my lord. At least – ' Mark Bolan made a show of hesitating, then shook his head. 'No, it couldn't be because of a little thing like that. I can't believe anybody'd be so mean. So spiteful.'

Tom stiffened and looked at Anna, frowning. She shook her head in bewilderment.

'Let us be the judge of that,' the Yellow Lord said.

'Well, the day before, I'd bumped into her in the playground. By accident, see? I was chasing one of my friends and didn't see her. . . .I didn't bump into her hard but she overbalanced and stepped into a puddle and got her new shoes dirty. I said sorry but she yelled at me she'd get even. "See if I don't get my own back!" she said.'

'That's not true!' Anna burst out. 'He's lying. I never saw him before he broke the vase! I didn't!'

The companions stared at her in silence. They didn't believe her.

'I haven't got any new shoes!' she shouted. 'He made the whole thing up!'

'I can vouch for that,' Lindy said, leaning forward in her mask like the moon rising. 'Look at her feet. She's been wearing those shabby old sneakers all summer. And there wasn't any puddle that day. I know. I was with Anna in the playground and it was as dry as a bone. I didn't see that boy either. Take him away,' she said, with a lordly wave of her hand, 'he's a liar.'

20

The companions burst out laughing. Mark Bolan was not popular. Shouts of 'Take the liar away!' drowned out the Yellow Lord's objections.

In the clamour, the shrill note of the recorder went unnoticed. The Herald blew out his cheeks until they became as red as his mask, but in vain. Angrily, the Goldmaster stood up, snatched the recorder out of the boy's hands and broke it in two.

Though the crack of the breaking wood was not loud, everyone was now silent.

'That's better,' he said, throwing the broken pieces on to the floor. 'Remember this is a court of justice, not a circus.'

The effect of this remark was somewhat spoiled by the fact that the Herald was shuffling round the throne on all fours like a dog, trying to find the second half of his broken recorder. The companions exchanged glances, putting up their hands to muffle their laughter.

'What got into him?' Tom whispered, staring at the Goldmaster in amazement.

'Wine,' Anna told him. She had noticed with dismay how often the silver cup had been refilled. 'If he goes on like this, he'll be too drunk to hear your speech. It'll all be wasted.'

Now the Goldmaster had turned on Lindy.

'And as for you,' he said, 'I've already warned you. Keep quiet until it's your turn to speak. If the Lord Defender wants to call you as a witness, that's up to him. Until then, keep your stupid mouth shut.'

'Yes, Goldmaster.'

It was a meek enough reply, but everybody knew that, behind her mask, the Silver Lady was smirking like a cat. You could hear the purr in her creamy voice. You could see it in the way she tilted her head and gazed up at the ceiling. Several companions looked up too, as if expecting to find the ceiling covered with the graffiti of her mocking thoughts.

The Goldmaster sat down again heavily, and held out his silver cup towards the Blue companion. Tom watched the boy fill it and step back into the shadows behind the throne. The Yellow Lord was speaking, trying to undo the damage Lindy had done to his witness. Under the cover of his voice, Tom moved over to the boy and whispered:

'A pound for you if you lose that bottle.'

'Lose it, my lord?' the boy asked, glancing nervously towards the Goldmaster.

'Not so loud. Yes. Empty it down the sink. Pour it on the floor. Anything you like.'

'It's no good, my lord,' the boy said. 'There's more bottles, crates of them in the storeroom. I can't lose them all.'

'No. Here's ten pence to keep quiet about it,' Tom said, handing over a coin. He moved away.

He was just in time. The Yellow Lord had finished. Tom stepped forward quickly.

'Just a minute! I have some questions for you,' he told Mark Bolan.

Mark, who'd been about to go, looked at him sullenly.

'I told everything I know,' he said.

'Yes. Yes, I'm sure you did your best,' Tom agreed with a pleasant smile. 'I know you're a loyal member of the Som and want to help the court. Just as I do. We all have our parts to play, even if they're not the ones we'd have chosen for ourselves.' He made a rueful face. It was as if he'd said, 'I didn't want to defend a traitor. You and I are really on the same side.'

Anna stared at him, her eyes huge and disbelieving. A whisper ruffled through the companions like wind in the grass. Mark Bolan smirked.

'Yes, my lord. Just as you say.'

'The only thing that troubles me,' Tom went on, 'is this business with the puddle and the new shoes. I know it's only a trifle, but people might say – "if he got that wrong, perhaps he got the whole lot wrong."'

'I only muddled the days for a minute. It was the Monday, not the Tuesday. It rained Monday morning, see? As for the shoes, anyone'd have thought they must be new, the fuss she made.'

'Yes, of course,' Tom said soothingly. 'I wasn't accusing you of lying. You're a deputy leader. Respected. . . . However, if your memory's so bad – '

146

'It's not, my lord!'

'There are other witnesses, you know.'

'Five of them,' Mark said gleefully. 'And they'll all say the same as me.'

'You've discussed it with them, then?'

Mark hesitated, half sensing a trap. But Tom was glancing down at some papers in his hand, looking bored, and Anna was slumped in misery on her stool, her head down, looking at nobody.

'I might've done,' he said cautiously. 'Why shouldn't I?'

'Some people might think it unwise. They might suspect collusion – '

'Objection!' the Lord of the Yellow cried. 'Goldmaster – '

'Objection sustained,' the Goldmaster said sleepily.

'I'll withdraw that remark,' Tom said easily. 'I apologise.' He turned again to Mark Bolan. 'I didn't mean for a moment to suggest that you'd coached the other five witnesses. However, if they're all going say exactly the same as you, it seems a waste of time to call them. Luckily, there was a sixth witness. No, I don't mean the prisoner,' he added, as Mark glanced across at Anna, who was now sitting up, watching them. 'Had you forgotten the Silver Lady was there?'

'Oh.' It was obvious to everybody that Mark had indeed forgotten the Silver Lady and was now wishing her at the bottom of the deep blue sea.

'Let's see how good your memory is,' Tom went on. 'When Miss Chivers turned round and saw the broken vase, what did she say?'

'She said, "What have you done now, Peter Elkin?"'

'Quite correct. And then?'

'She – the prisoner – she said I done it.'

'Right away? I understood she said something else first.'

Mark Bolan glanced at the Silver Lady and muttered, 'I can't remember everything.'

'No. So it seems. Let me help you,' Tom said. 'As I heard it, the accused said, "He didn't! He didn't break the vase!"'

'She might've done.'

'And what did you say to that? Or is your memory so bad that you can't even remember what you said yourself?'

'I can, then! I said, "Yes, he did," and she says, "Oo, you liar. You broke it yourself. I saw you." And that's God's truth!' he ended triumphantly.

'And that's God's truth,' Tom repeated softly. He was silent for a moment, smiling. Everybody watched him. Then he said, raising his voice so that it rang through the room, 'My lords, I ask you to note that by this witness's own admission, Anna Cotman did not betray him, did not even mention his name, until *after* he himself had accused, falsely accused a young companion. Only then did she feel impelled to speak out. To tell the truth and shame the devil. He – ' Tom pointed at Mark Bolan ' – in her eyes, he was the traitor!'

'Objection!' the Lord of the Yellow shouted. 'Goldmaster, you can't allow this!'

'Can't allow it,' the Goldmaster agreed, shaking his

head. 'Objection sus – sus – you know, whatever it is.' He leaned forward and wagged his finger at Tom. 'Can't have you browbeating my witness, you know.'

'*Your* witness,' Lindy said. 'You're supposed to be impartial. Not intoxicated,' she added unwisely.

The Goldmaster got to his feet and stood swaying, like an angry snake. 'I warned you! I warned you!' he shouted. 'Guards!' He tried to click his fingers, but they must have been damp for they made no noise. This irritated him further and he yelled at the top of his voice, 'Throw her out!'

Nobody moved to carry out his bidding. Lindy, though small and skinny, younger than all the lords and most of the companions, had gained a reputation that made people wary of her. 'She's full of dirty tricks,' they said. 'She'll get her own back one day when you least expect it.' So they stared at her uneasily and hoped someone else would be fool enough to take her on.

'Throw her out!' the Goldmaster cried again, his voice cracking with anger.

Still nobody moved.

'Do I have to do it myself?' he asked, looking round him in disbelief.

'No. Let me.' The Lord of the Yellow came forward.

'There's no need for anyone to interfere,' Lindy said quickly, tossing her head. 'I've no intention of staying where I'm not wanted. I was going, anyway.' She got up and made her way to the door. As she passed in front of the throne, she said softly:

'You wait!'

The Lord of the Yellow was quick as lightning striking. He gripped her by the shoulder and spun her round to face him. The calm, unchanging smiles on both the silver and the yellow masks made his words sound all the more frightening.

'Remember your oath, Silver Lady. You break it and it'll be your death.'

'I won't break it,' she whimpered. He let go of her and she ran across the room and disappeared through the door.

21

The Lord of the Yellow clapped his hands and shouted for silence.

'The court will adjourn,' he said. 'Companions, keep your places. Your leaders will bring you refreshments.'

What now? Anna wondered. Surely they can't just be stopping for a tea break? Perhaps with Mark Bolan discredited, they'll put him in the dock and let me go.

But as the lords began making their way into the storeroom, Tom hurried over to her and she saw at once from his face that he had no good news for her.

'Listen,' he said, his voice so low that she could hardly hear him, 'I have to go with them. I'll do my best but — Anna, if you get a chance, try and slip away. Go straight home — '

'What? *Why?*'

'It's no good. It's not going to work. Jeremy's too far gone. I wish I'd never let you come here. Now Lindy's left — '

Before he could say any more, two of the new lords came up, one on either side of him.

'The Goldmaster wants you, Defender,' they said.

'I won't be a minute.'

'He wants you now. Right away.'

Tom hesitated, glancing at Anna. He looked young and defenceless without a mask, standing between the two tall figures in their purple and orange robes. She could see that he was worried and uncertain what to do.

'Goodbye, then,' she said, trying to smile.

Their arithmetic had gone wrong. Four lords for her and four against, with the Goldmaster and the Silver Lady cancelling each other out. But Lindy had gone. The odds were against them now.

I'm not going to cry, she thought. They can't kill me, can they?

The deputy leaders had come back with trays loaded with tins of coke and beer and shandy, packets of biscuits and bags of crisps. The companions crowded round them. She saw Mark Bolan. He was standing with his back to her. He had a tin in one hand and was shaking it vigorously. Then he pulled out the metal tab. A jet of dark liquid shot up to the ceiling and rained down on him and his friends, who shrieked with laughter. They were just boys fooling. They didn't look dangerous.

But she remembered how they had chanted, stamping their feet on the floor. How they had yelled at her and called her traitor, their faces ugly with hate. She was terribly afraid.

Nobody seemed to be watching her. She slipped off her stool and sat on the edge of the table, looking round. Immediately the Red Herald came up to her.

'I was only stretching my legs,' she said quickly.

'Walk around a bit, why don't you? Want some coke?' he asked, holding out a tin.

The unexpected kindness almost made her cry. 'Thanks.'

'He shouldn't've broken my recorder,' the boy said, as if to excuse his generosity. 'The Red Lord said to tell you you got friends.'

'I know. I'm grateful.'

'Got enemies too, though.' He paused and glanced round the room. A few companions were watching them. He lowered his voice. 'Got a message for you from him. He says you're to make a run for it.'

'But – '

'Don't argue. Walk this way, slowly, like there was nothing on your mind. There're guards at the front. You'll have to go the back way, through the store-room – don't look at the door! They're watching us. We'll just stroll up and down in the shadows. Make like you're asking me something and I'm shaking my head. When the lords start coming back, see you're near the door – *don't look at it*! Soon as they've passed, you slip in and out the back door and run like a rabbit. Worth a try.'

'Won't you get into trouble? They've seen you with me.'

'He shouldn't've broken my recorder. It was a good one. Cost a lot.'

'He'll buy you another one.'

'I don't want another one. I liked the one I had. It was special, see? I played my first solo at the . . . Ssh! Here they come. Good luck!' he said, and walked away.

Anna shrank back in the shadows and watched the lords walk past. The old lords came first and went silently to their places. Then the new lords sauntered in with the Goldmaster, laughing and talking together. The Lord of the Yellow was not among them.

Tom came next. He didn't glance round but he must have known she was there because he stopped in just the right position to shield her from the person standing in the doorway.

'Have you many more witnesses, Lord Accuser?' he asked, but it was no good. The Lord of the Yellow had seen Anna, had been looking out for her from the moment he reached the doorway.

'Guards!' he called, and they came running, Mark Bolan and one of his friends. 'Put the prisoner back in her place. And another time, keep your eyes open. If she'd got away, I'd have put you in the dock.'

'Dickory, dickory, dock,' the Goldmaster said, giggling foolishly. 'The mouse ran away from the clock. Can't have that. Bad for discipline. Got to make an example. . . .' He stopped in front of Anna and touched her cheek lightly with his hand. 'Pity it had to be you,' he said.

The lords led him back to his throne and the guards put Anna back on her table. The trial went on.

The next five witnesses were the boys who had been with Mark Bolan when the vase was broken. They all told the same tale, word for word, as he had said they would. The companions fidgeted and yawned. The Goldmaster, lolling back on his cushions, seemed to have gone to sleep. Even the Lord Defender, cross-examining, sounded bored.

Only one boy listened to every word, trembling. 'I'll only call you if I have to,' he'd been promised. 'If things go badly. . . .'

But things always went badly for him. He'd been born unlucky. Everything he did went wrong. The one person who'd made him feel his luck had changed was now sitting perched on a table, stuck there for all eyes to see, reviled as a traitor.

I should've stayed in bed, he thought. I won't do her any good. I'll only let her down again.

Then he heard the words he had been dreading.

'For my first witness,' the Lord Defender said loudly. 'I call the companion known as Yellow Shrimp.'

Other voices took it up, 'Calling Yellow Shrimp! Calling Yellow Shrimp!' Heads turned, looking for him.

He couldn't move. The Red companions, who had brought him and kept him hidden until now, prodded him and muttered at him, but it was no good. His legs would not obey him.

'Calling Yellow Shrimp!'

'No!' Anna shouted. 'Leave him alone! I didn't want him to be called. I told you, Tom. Let him go home.'

At the sound of her voice, Peter Elkin stood up. Helped, pushed and shoved by the Red companions, he made his way to the centre aisle, and stood, shaking. Tears blurred his vision, shimmering in his wet eyes, hiding the staring faces.

'Go home, Peter!' Anna called. 'It's all right. We don't need you. Go home!'

But he walked forwards. Warm hands met him and guided him behind the witness chair. Someone muttered, 'Well done, Shrimp.'

'Objection!' a voice shouted. It was the voice he hated, the voice of his lord. 'Goldmaster, this witness is one of my companions. I was told he was ill, deliberately prevented from seeing him. Now they've smuggled him in here, disguised in a red mask. I demand that he be dismissed.'

'Nonsense! I've the right to call any witness I please – '

The two lords were shouting. Peter shrank and turned towards Anna. She was looking at him, her eyes dark and bright. She said something. He thought it was 'You shouldn't have come.'

'I wanted to,' he said. 'I'm glad I did.' And this at least was true.

The Goldmaster sat up with a jerk, and turned his shining face from one shouting lord to the other, but said nothing.

'Jeremy, wake up!' Tom shouted. 'For God's sake, wake up. We wanted the Som to be something fine, remember? You said we'd fight evil. Here's your evil!' He pointed at the Lord of the Yellow. 'I accuse this lord of corrupting his companions. I accuse him of forcing them to steal for him. This witness will tell you – '

'Look out, Tom! He's got a knife!' Anna screamed.

Leaping to her feet, she picked up the stool and threw it at the Lord of the Yellow. She missed.

But at least the Yellow Lord, in dodging away, gave Tom time to snatch up the witness chair. He held it in front of him like a shield, the legs pointing outwards. 'Run! Anna! Peter! Run for it!' he commanded, not taking his eyes off the Lord of the Yellow.

Anna jumped down from the table and circled behind it, watching them. Peter had gone. The Lord of the Yellow held his knife in his right hand, the blade pointing upwards, gleaming like water. He crouched, keeping just out of Tom's reach, waiting his moment. Tom stood poised, his unmasked face pale and watchful.

Anna ran to the throne. 'Jeremy, stop them. Tom's your friend! He'll kill him. You've got to stop them!'

'What's happening? What's he doing with that chair?' the Goldmaster asked. 'Is it the games? Whose side are you on? I know you, don't I?'

Anna stared at him, then turned away hopelessly. Someone began to chant softly, 'Som – som – som,' and others took it up. Louder and louder it sounded. They were on their feet now, making a circle round the two lords.

The Lord of the Yellow darted forward and caught hold of the chair with his left hand. They struggled, each trying to wrest it away from the other. There was a loud crack as the chair broke, leaving Tom with only the back strut to defend himself with. The Lord of the Yellow gave a great shout of triumph.

Anna screamed, snatched a cushion from the

throne and ran forwards as he lunged, catching the blade of his knife with it. A ripping sound, a cloud of white feathers – and then he had pulled the knife free.

'No!' somebody shouted, and as if following a signal, everybody began fighting. Figures struggled in the flickering light. Candle-jars were knocked over and rolled across the concrete floor, tripping unwary feet. Somebody crashed into the throne, nearly knocking the Goldmaster off his cushions. He clung to the arms with both hands, and stared silently in front of him as his kingdom collapsed into chaos. Everywhere his followers struggled and panted and grunted on the floor. Behind his golden mask, he began to weep.

22

'What mischief are you up to, Lindy?' Harry King asked.

They were walking briskly in the late afternoon sunlight, the short, sallow man and his skinny step-daughter. He had turned his head towards her and the light reflected in his glasses, hiding the expression in his eyes.

'I'm not up to any mischief,' she said. 'Actually, I'm doing something good, though no one's going to believe that. I don't expect to be thanked. They'll say I did it out of spite because I was cross with him, but I didn't. At least, not altogether,' she added with one of her sudden flashes of honesty. These always disarmed him, coming so unexpectedly from a character that seemed to him to be otherwise a mass of affectations.

'It is really,' she said with satisfaction, 'very noble of me.'

She was feeling pleased with herself. When she had left the trial, she had run all the way to Harry's office, not really expecting to find him there, for he had other offices besides the small one in Redmarsh. Finding him was like a tick of approval from God.

'You've got to come with me, Harry,' she'd said, to the secret amusement of his clerk. 'Quickly. We need you. Jeremy needs you,' she'd added, knowing full well whom he loved the most.

'What's happened? Is he hurt?'

'No, not the way you mean. There's trouble.'

She refused to say any more, shaking her head to his questions and putting on her most stubborn expression. Without arguing further, he'd picked up his jacket, said a brief word to his clerk and come with her.

His car was parked round the corner in Park Street.

'Do up your seat belt,' he told her. 'Where is he? At home?'

'No. Go to the old workshop. W. H. Briggs and Son.' Seeing he looked blank, she said, 'You gave it to us. Well, you gave us the keys. Don't you remember?'

'The old workshop in Rede Street ...? Yes, I remember now. I told Jeremy he could use it. *What's happened*?'

'Nothing, not when I left. But I think you ought to come. I think you should've come earlier,' she said reprovingly. 'If we'd been my kids, I'd have kept an eye on us. But of course, you're only our stepfather, so I suppose it didn't matter to you.'

'What's happened? Lindy, please tell me.'

'I can't,' she said, wriggling in her seat. 'I've sworn a most dreadful oath of secrecy.'

'Oh, those dreadful oaths of childhood,' he said with a brief smile. 'I swore dozens of them in my time, and broke them all. I'd have thought you were too sensible to believe in such things.'

'But this is a truly horrible one. I made it up myself.'

'Then you must know it's nonsense.'

She said nothing for a moment, looking out of the window, her face thoughtful. 'Everybody else believes it,' she said at last.

'More fool they.' He glanced at her, then added. 'Not us. You and I are clever, Lindy. Too clever to believe in superstition –'

'Too clever to be flattered into doing something I don't want to do!' she said sharply, and he laughed.

They were nearly there. As they turned into Rede Street, she said quickly:

'Harry, don't you think we should take someone with us?'

'What do you mean?'

'I don't know. Not the police. Some men, anyone strong. He's not alone. There's a lot of them there. Forty or fifty, I didn't count.'

'You don't have to come in with me.'

'It was you I was thinking of,' she said crossly. 'After all, you're only a small man.'

To her surprise, he smiled and said, 'Thank you, Lindy. I'll be all right.' They drew up outside the old workshop. 'Stay in the car,' he said. 'I promise to shout if I need help.'

Still smiling, he turned and went into the workshop, brushing aside the guard who had been sitting on the doorstep, reading a comic.

* * *

Nobody saw Harry King come into the Hall of Secrets. The light from the opening door went unnoticed. He shut it behind him, and stood for a moment, letting his eyes adjust to the candle-light. It was very dark. Many of the candles had gone out. He saw a jar rolling towards him and stopped it with his foot. At the other end of the room, a figure was sitting on a kind of throne, stiff and unreal as a golden idol. There were candle-jars on the tables on either side of him. The rest of the room was in shadow, and noisy with obscure scufflings and thumps.

'What the devil is going on?' he said.

He was a small man, but thickset, and his voice was loud enough when he wanted it to be. There was an immediate silence and he saw pale blurs in the shadows as faces turned to look at him.

'Why don't you have some light in here?' he asked impatiently, and crossing briskly to one of the windows, began struggling to get the rough wooden shutter down. He heard murmurs behind him and soft footfalls and the hair prickled on the back of his neck.

'Be careful. They've got knives,' a voice whispered out of the darkness.

I should've listened to Lindy, he thought. Is this the end of Harry King?

Then the shutter came down in his hands, and he swung round, holding it in front of him, much as Tom had held the stool. Daylight streamed through the dusty window on to figures in tawdry robes and gaudy masks. It fell on the dirty floor, littered with empty tins and crumpled bags, cigarette ends and, of all things, a drift of white feathers. What in hell's name had been going on here? Right in front of him were the figures he'd been warned about, four of them hooded and robed in different colours, yellow and purple, orange and turquoise. Three of them held knives in their hands and one a bottle.

Now for it, Harry, he thought grimly.

But they did not come at him. In fact, they shrank back, blinking as if the light hurt them. Behind them, there was a soft scurrying, a patter of running feet. The companions were deserting them, running out of both doors, tearing off their masks and throwing them away as they ran down the street.

'I should put those knives away,' Harry said quietly. 'Someone might get hurt.'

For a moment it still hung in the balance. Then the one holding the bottle dropped it on to the floor and turned to run. The others followed him, putting away their knives, blundering across the room in their long robes, their feet kicking aside the fallen candle-jars.

Harry made no attempt to stop them. Then he saw with horror that Lindy was standing in the doorway they were making for.

'Stand back, Lindy!' he shouted, running towards her.

She stayed where she was, staring. The figure in yellow barged into her, knocking her out of the way. Her hand shot out as she fell back, and tore off his mask. Then he and his fellows were gone.

'I saw him!' Lindy cried triumphantly, as Harry came up to her. 'I saw his face.'

'Who was it?'

'Nobody,' she said.

He could make no sense of this. 'Are you all right?' he asked.

'Yes.'

He turned and looked back into the long room. It was almost empty now. Over by the unshuttered window, a boy was sitting on the floor. He was wearing a green robe but no mask, and his face was pale and smudged with blood. He was cradling one arm in his lap and the green sleeve was heavily splotched with dark stains and the hand that supported it was red. Beside him, a girl was kneeling. At first he did not recognise her as Lindy's pretty little friend, so white was her face and so huge her frightened eyes.

'Tom – Tom, are you all right? Oh, you're not dead!'

'He doesn't look dead to me,' Harry said, coming up. 'Why don't you fetch him a drink of water?'

She got to her feet and ran off.

Harry knelt down beside the boy. There was something vaguely familiar about him – yes, of course, an old friend of Jeremy's – what had the girl called him? Tom, that was it.

'Let's see the damage, Tom,' he said, gently lifting the sodden sleeve.

'It's not too bad,' Tom said.

'Bad enough. It'll need several stitches.' He got a clean hanky out of his pocket, doubled it into a pad and placed it on the wound. 'Were there any other casualties? The ones who ran away?'

'I don't know. I didn't see.'

'Never mind. Was it the one in yellow who cut you?'

'Yes.'

'I thought so. His was the only dirty blade. With luck, the others didn't use theirs.' He was silent for a moment, concentrating on tying his grey silk tie round the handkerchief on Tom's arm. The red stain came through almost at once.

'Use this,' Lindy said, holding out some yellow cloth. 'You can tear it. He won't be coming back for it.'

'Thanks.' He tore it into strips and bound up Tom's arm. Then he sat back on his heels and glanced towards the solitary figure on the throne. 'Now what's to be done?' he muttered, and sighed.

'You mustn't tell the police,' Lindy said. 'It wouldn't be fair. After all, in a way, it's all your fault. You'll have to hush it up, Harry. You know you can. Tom doesn't have to go to hospital. We can bathe his arm with Dettol and do it up properly when we get home – '

'Hold on, Lindy! You said there were about fifty people here?'

'About that.'

'Too many,' Harry said, shaking his head. 'Someone will talk. Someone always does. And then we'd be in real trouble. No, you'd better leave this to me. I'll need to know exactly what's happened – '

They glanced at each other and then looked back at him. Neither of them spoke. Anna, coming up with water in the silver cup, stared at him with her round dark eyes.

'We can't,' she said. 'We can't tell you. We took an oath –'

'Oh, that stupid, childish oath,' Lindy said, tossing her head. 'I don't care about that. I'll tell you, Harry. I'm not superstitious and silly.'

'Good girl.'

When she had told him, he turned to look at the figure on the throne. It was curled up now, its head buried in its hands. He sighed, and getting up, walked over and stood for a moment looking down at the Goldmaster. Then he lifted the lowered head and removed the golden mask.

'It's time to face up to things now, son,' he said.

23

Tom and Anna came to say goodbye to Jeremy and to wish him luck. They did not go into the house but stood outside on the pavement with Lindy, and watched him go off in Harry's Rolls Royce, a glimpse of a pale face at the window. No smile for the watchers, no wave of the hand.

It had been a mistake to come. He hadn't wanted them. Had stared at them blankly when he saw them, and turned away, saying fretfully to Harry, 'For God's sake, let's go.' He'd looked terrible.

They watched the car out of sight.

'It's supposed to be a very good place he's going to,' Lindy said. 'The best. Harry saw to that. But he says it won't be easy for Jeremy. He says there's no easy way. . . .'

They were silent for a moment, thinking of Jeremy, for whom things had always been easy before. Even the hated stepfather, being rich, had been a sugared pill to swallow. And now Harry was the one he turned to, the only one he could bear to see him.

'I'm sorry, I'd ask you in,' Lindy said, 'but Mum's crying, and she can't bear people to see her with her face all blotchy. Not even me. She won't want me to try and comfort her so I might as well go out. Come on, you two, I'll treat you to an ice-cream at the Bluebell Café. Harry gave me some money.'

'Thirty pieces of silver?' Tom asked.

She turned on him in a blaze of anger.

'I'm not a Judas! I didn't betray Jeremy. His friends did, and I don't just mean the Lord of the Yellow and his creeps. I mean *you*, Tom Smith! You must've known he'd started on drugs, you're not thick. But you couldn't bring yourself to tell tales, not you, you're far too superior. You'd rather let him rot than dirty your lily-white soul. Well, I wouldn't! He's my brother and I'm fond of him, even if he is a bleeding ass. I'd break a hundred promises to save him. I'd tell a thousand lies. Harry understands. Harry thanked me. He said if it had gone on much longer, it'd have been too late for Jeremy – if it's not too late already.'

She turned and ran away from them, blinded by angry tears. She was alone again. Harry had taken Jeremy away to an expensive bin, her mother was crying by herself and Tom and Anna were together. Laughing probably. Nobody wanted *her*.

I don't care, she thought, racing down Swan Street and on to the common. I hate them all. I hate everybody in the world – except perhaps Harry. He and I are the same kind. Nobody likes him either. And poor Jeremy, I don't hate him.

She stopped, out of breath, and leaned her forehead against a tree trunk. The thought of her brother made her cry again. Poor Jeremy, who had broken down when the Som was destroyed, had shut himself in his room and refused to come out or speak to anybody.

Harry had said there was a good chance he'd be all right in time, but how long? How long would he be away?

'Lindy! Lindy!'

She stiffened and turned her head a little, trying to see right round the corner of her eye. It was Anna's voice. Did she really want Anna? Sweet Anna whom everybody liked? Well, perhaps not everybody. The new lords hadn't liked her. The Som had fought over her and destroyed itself. Nobody, she thought, has ever fought over me.

'Lindy!' Anna cried again, skidding to a halt by the tree. And standing there, panting, her curls tumbled and her cheeks flushed, looking horribly pretty.

'What do you want?' Lindy asked coldly.

'Let's be friends,' Anna said.

Nobody had ever said that to Lindy before. Always she'd been the one to say it, to make the first move, to demand friendship and somehow lose it again. A smile spread over her face, sweet as jam. Somebody wanted her. Somebody had come running after her, risking blisters and a stitch in the side, all for her! It might be only old Anna but she was better than nothing. Much better, Lindy decided, looking at her friend's smiling face. In fact, you couldn't really find a better friend than Anna if you looked the whole world over.

'I know what you want. You're after that free ice-cream,' she said. 'OK. Come on.'

As they walked together over the common, Lindy told Anna what had happened since the day of the trial. Harry had seen to everything –

'He wanted you and me kept out of it. You know what his story is, don't you?' she asked.

'Tom told me,' Anna said. 'He said Harry told the doctors at the hospital that there'd been a fancy dress party and it'd got out of hand. Something about gate-crashers and one of them pulling a knife when Jeremy tried to keep them out, wasn't that it?'

'Clever, wasn't it? He called them an undesirable element – don't you think that's a good name for the Lord of the Yellow? He said none of us had any idea who they were, as they were hooded and masked.'

'So they'll get away with it?'

'I don't know. Harry may do something. . . . I think he knows who they are but he wouldn't tell me. He said he'd made a bargain with Jeremy and he wasn't going to break it, because Jeremy needed something firm to hang on to. Harry says there's a time to break promises and a time to keep them and you have to be clever to know which is which. I don't think you'd better start breaking yours, Anna. You'd be sure to get it wrong.'

Anna only smiled at this. She was more sure of herself. She wouldn't be easy to boss around any more.

'You saw him, didn't you, Lindy?' she asked. 'The Lord of the Yellow, I mean. When you snatched his mask off, you must've seen his face.'

'Yes.'

'What was he like?' Anna said.

Her eyes were huge. She looked like someone prepared to hear marvels. Lindy was tempted to say he'd had horns and a twisted nose and green eye-brows. Then she decided the truth was even odder.

'He was nothing special. You wouldn't look at him twice if you saw him in the street. I doubt if I'd even recognise him again. Don't you think that's a frightening thought?'

Anna was silent for a minute, thinking it out.

'You mean he might be anybody and we wouldn't know?'

'Right. He didn't look evil. Just weak. You know – like if he said boo to a goose, the goose would just shrug and walk on. Yet he had only to put on a mask and we were all scared of him. Funny, isn't it? He'd never have become so powerful if we'd seen his real face. It just shows something or other.'

'Why did he wear gloves?'

'Dunno. Perhaps he had a missing finger. Or leprosy. Or a tattoo. Or maybe his hands were cold.'

'I think it was because – ' Anna broke off. She was looking past Lindy. Her face brightened and she smiled. Turning, Lindy saw Tom running towards them.

'Go away!' she shouted.

But he had come to apologise. 'I'm sorry, Lindy,' he said. 'I shouldn't have said that. It was stupid of me. And unfair. Perhaps you're right. Perhaps I should've told – but I didn't know for certain. I only guessed. And – and we've always covered up for each other, Jeremy and I, ever since we were kids. I don't know. I don't know what I should've done. It isn't easy, is it?'

'No,' Lindy agreed. 'It wasn't easy.'

She did not want to quarrel with him any more. He was Jeremy's friend and he'd said that she might have been right, and that comforted her. Perhaps one day Jeremy would understand and forgive her.

'Come and have an ice-cream with us,' she said.

They walked on slowly, talking at first quietly and solemnly. But then a small dog, coming wet and muddy from the river, started jumping up at them, and soon they were shouting and laughing together.

It was a beautiful day, warm and soft and smelling of grass. Anna wanted to run and jump for joy. It was all over. For so long she'd been cut off from everybody, from Gran and the teachers at school and the people in the streets. The Som had imprisoned her in a shadowy world of secrecy, a world in which hidden horrors moved, and she'd been unable to cry for help. She was free at last. They were all free. Lindy and Tom and little Peter Elkin and Red. The herald could buy another recorder and the companions could play their games in the open air, and they'd never have to go to the Hall of Secrets again. The whole bright everyday world was theirs.

But not Jeremy's. Not yet.

ALSO BY VIVIEN ALCOCK

The Haunting of Cassie Palmer

'You believe in spirits yourself! I know you do!'
'Not any more I don't.'
'All right then Cassie Palmer, prove it. You're the gifted one. Let's see what you can do, O seventh child of a seventh child! Nothing to be scared of if you don't believe in it. And if it doesn't work, you'll know you're normal like us.'

Taunted and angry, Cassie calls to the spirits and an angry and fearsome spirit responds. Deverill stands before her at the gravestone – the haunting has begun.